MORE MURDER IN A NUNNERY

Two years after the murder of a wealthy Baroness inside Harrington Convent, the orderly everyday affairs of the nuns and students are disrupted anew with unmitigated misfortune. When a body neatly wrapped in brown paper is found by the gardener, Mr. Turtle, on his rubbish heap, the police are again summoned to the Convent, led by Mr. Pearson, now Deputy Commissioner. Can he successfully negotiate his way through the colourful cast of characters to find the culprit?

ERIC SHEPHERD

MORE MURDER IN A NUNNERY

Complete and Unabridged

LINFORD
Leicester

First published in Great Britain in 1954

First Linford Edition
published 2019

A catalogue record for this book is available
from the British Library.

ISBN 978–1–4448–3986–9

Published by
F. A. Thorpe (Publishing)
Anstey, Leicestershire

Set by Words & Graphics Ltd.
Anstey, Leicestershire
Printed and bound in Great Britain by
T. J. International Ltd., Padstow, Cornwall

This book is printed on acid-free paper

To
FRIEDA

Author's Note

The characters in this story may be described as plausible fictions. They are certainly fictions; it is the author's hope that they may also be found plausible.

Time is a mode of thought. It is the author's request that readers will so modify their thought that the events of this book shall seem to take place exactly two years after those of *Murder in a Nunnery*.

E.S.

1

History Repeats Itself at Harrington Convent

When Reverend Mother of Harrington was told that another dead body had been found on the conventual premises she was silent for, possibly, ten seconds.

Then she said: 'And they say history never repeats itself —'

Mother Assistant, her informant, underwent a spasm of those strongly aquiline features which, though she was the gentlest soul, struck the Junior School as with a palsy.

'I cannot *express*, dear Reverend Mother, my sympathy —'

'Let me know the worst.'

'It isn't the *worst*, thank God. Not one of the children. Not one of us. Only a man —'

God frequently consoled Reverend Mother in strange ways. He did so now.

But not a sign of this interior consolation showed on her face.

'Tell me,' was all she said, 'about this man.'

The facts of the matter may be condensed as follows:

The dead body of a man, a perfect stranger, had been found early that morning by Mr. Turtle (the Convent's head-gardener and, in a general way, most unhandy man), upon, of all places, his own sacred rubbish-dump.

This dump, if dump it could be called, was as close to Mr. Turtle's heart as anything could be to that remote organ. It was built with the greatest discrimination and maintained with the utmost method. It was a thing of beauty and, to its maker, a joy for ever — so much so that he was used to begin the day by going and having a prolonged and profoundly self-satisfied stare at it.

This he had been doing that morning when he saw what looked like a very large brown-paper parcel placed on top of the dump so as to impair the perfect symmetry of its construction.

A man of deep but controlled feelings, he had suppressed his indignation and hurried to the spot, strongly suspecting that 'some o' them Convent young lidies, I don't think' had been up to their tricks again.

'It were the queerest parcel as ever I seen, mum.'

On attempting to lift the parcel Mr. Turtle had stumbled and fallen under its weight. The brown-paper swathings had come undone, disclosing a 'body' — the body of a man.

It was 'nobody as I known, mum, and I will not deny that a weakness come over me strength, like. A nice thing for a man to find on a empty stommick, and at a convent, mind you. It was with difficulty as I *retrace* me steps where a cup of 'ot tea do somethink to restore me faculties. I seen at once, mum, as a dead body was a matter for you lidies. I ain't sayin' a word agin nobody, but if you *will* 'ave furriners a-workin' on the place and 'inderin' rather than 'elpin', then dead bodies a-croppin' up promiscous is no more than you had ought to expec'.'

This allusion of Mr. Turtle's referred to the employment by the Convent of a Spaniard to act as aide to himself in the kitchen-gardens. Green-fingered as Juan Copanza undoubtedly was, bright, intelligent and a hard worker, nothing could palliate to Mr. Turtle his dark complexion and broken English, or the fact that he had been taken on in place of Mr. Turtle's own son 'Mock' (so called by the School) on the latter's 'doin' better for 'isself'.

'Dead 'e was,' Mr. Turtle had reported to Mother Assistant; 'dead, and gone to 'is account. Which, mum, asking your pardon, so must we all, flesh bein' like grass, and the man wot thinketh 'e stand apt to come a nasty cropper at the 'ands of an orl-seein' God.'

Reverend Mother's face, as she listened to this recital, had undergone certain fleeting changes. Not that she smiled, or committed herself in any way. But there was a feeling, somehow, that if a dead body *had* to be found at the Convent, then on top of Mr. Turtle's dump was the place where she could bear it best.

Reverend Mother and Mr. Turtle had

4

never been soul-mates.

Once mistress of the facts, Reverend Mother proceeded to the situation.

'The police must be informed at once. Will you attend to that, Mother?' And, guessing from certain movements of the aquiline features what was going on in Mother Assistant's mind, she added:

'I mean the ordinary police — at the Harrington station. I'm afraid it's no use dialling 999 and expecting Mr. Pearson to grow on the doorstep.'

'Oh no, of course not, Reverend Mother.'

Chief-Inspector Andrew Pearson was that great luminary of the Yard who had come to the Convent's aid on the occasion of the stabbing of old Baroness Sliema, and had shown such tact and delicacy, and handled the matter so successfully, that he was remembered as a very Bayard by the Community, and was never out of its prayers.

Reverend Mother knew best, of course. That went without saying. Mother Assistant professed no knowledge of the police and their elaborate etiquette. But she was a very much disappointed woman when the oracle was spoken and she found that immediate recourse to Mr. Pearson was by no means to be had. The 'ordinary' police! And Mother Assistant felt so sure that Mr. Pearson would want to help Harrington again.

Nevertheless Mother Assistant was every inch (and she stood well up to six foot) a nun, and was off in discharge of her distasteful duty without a further word.

One opening of the door served both to let Mother Assistant out and to let Mother Peagle in.

The latter's appearance could not have been more timely. Mother Peagle was headmistress of the School, that super-sensitive organism which must always be given first place in all practical consider-ations. Reverend Mother, a consummate mistress of the spared word, put the facts, and Mother Peagle listened with that impassivity of countenance which long dealing with girls had perfected in her.

'I understand, Reverend Mother. The children need know nothing of this. I had better put the kitchen-gardens out of bounds at once. With your permission, I will go now and do so.'

Reverend Mother had but to incline her head, and a few minutes later a notice in Mother Peagle's blackest-lettered hand was posted on the board, and the Head of the School — one Miss Torquilla Rohays, famous for her biceps — was under summons, as were all the 'Blue Ribbons' or prefects, to wait upon Mother Peagle at recess.

Hardly had Mother Peagle fixed her notice and gone her way when a girl seemed to slip out of nowhere and stealthily approach the board. She moved with extraordinary speed and absolute silence. Mother Peagle's lettered hand was very black and large indeed. A single glance of the girl's eyes as she passed seemed sufficient, and she slipped again into invisibility.

But why did she wring her hands? And who was she that made so un-English a gesture?

2

From the Police Angle

It is extraordinary how different the same thing may appear from an altered point of view.

The body on the dump, which appeared to the Convent unmitigated misfortune, struck the police in quite a different way.

There had been of late in the police area of Harrington a prolonged period of unnatural civic virtue. Burglars seemed to have left the neighbourhood *en masse*. Even motorists, who can as a rule be relied on for a little furious driving, dropped to 20 m.p.h. around Harrington. The juvenile population seemed to have made a self-denying ordinance of the 'pictures' or at least suspended their efforts to practise the ethics so generally inculcated there. Miss Olive Churston, the young woman detective officer at

Harrington, sick as she was of petty larcenies, began to find that even the pettiest larceny is better than no larceny at all.

Eden, or the Reign of Innocence, seemed to have returned to Harrington. And this was very dull for the police.

The Superintendent was spoiling for a really tough job — preferably one involving 'toughs'. So were the sergeants to a man, and no less the P.C.s. Miss Churston, as has been said, was lamenting the loss of the light finger.

It was upon such police doldrums as these that Mother Assistant's telephone-call tinklingly intruded, and Sergeant Baseldon, who happened to be nearest to the instrument, positively skipped to answer.

'Is that the — er — Harrington police-station?'

'Yessir,' replied the Sergeant, and just refrained from springing sharply to attention.

The Sergeant had been in the Army, and he thought he knew that way of speaking. It was an officer, and an officer on whom he did not hesitate to confer field rank.

It was in fact the voice of Mother Assistant crouching in an agony of nervousness at her end of the wire. Telephoning always made Mother Assistant nervous, and when she was nervous her voice and manner reverted to that long line of military ancestors, including a field-marshal or two, of which she was sprung.

'I am speaking on behalf of the Reverend Mother of Harrington Convent of the Immaculate Conception —'

The Sergeant paled. To have to request a field-officer to repeat himself! But there was no alternative.

'Begging your pardon, sir, but might I ask you to say them words again?'

The field-rank officer appeared in a lenient mood. The words were repeated without a rebuke.

'Reverend Mother presents her compliments, and wishes to report a murder —'

The Sergeant reeled. The blood rushed violently to his head, and he all but dropped the receiver. But discipline told, and he rallied to reply.

'A murder. Yessir. Reverend Mother of Harrington Convent of the Immaculate Conception presents compliments, and wishes to report a — a murder —'

'Or so it would appear,' answered the voice, which astonished the Sergeant by its deep sternness and yet total absence of irascibility. 'At least, a — a dead body has been found in the kitchen-gardens —'

'A dead body, sir. Kitchen-gardens. Harrington Convent of the — hum, ha. Reverend Mother —'

The Sergeant rambled on incoherently, momentarily expecting to be called to order by some thunder-clap from the other end. But none came. Instead the stern voice put him in quiet possession of the facts and begged, again on behalf of Reverend Mother, that the police would give the matter their attention.

Only one request was made.

'You see, we are a school here. It is not desired that the children should — Reverend Mother is sure you will understand if she asks you to come to the *back* door and, to what extent this may be possible,

11

in *plain* clothes —'

'Very good, sir. Officers will report immediate, appropriate. Thank *you*, sir.'

But as the Sergeant hung up the receiver he felt considerable concern for the mental state of that field-officer.

'Shell-shock, I should say — poor fellow. Never a damn or a cuss or a 'go to hell!' Ah, it was sad to hear him —'

But the Sergeant soon cheered up as he hurried to spread the good news round the station. A murder! That was something like, that was. Make a new man of the Super, this would. This would show them fellas at Wimbledon and Putney and Barnes and Wandsworth who'd been going around sneering that Harrington was 'dead-alive'. This would show —

But at this point the Sergeant broke off to bestow a broad, a bright, a beaming and even affectionate smile on a young colleague, whom he also chucked under the chin, kissed with the utmost assurance, and addressed as 'poppet'.

'Hallo, poppet. Waiting round, like, to see if Uncle has any news? You bet your life!'

Olive Churston, for she it was, showed no surprise and certainly no resentment at this familiar treatment. Indeed, she put herself in the way of more of it by going and standing beside the Sergeant with her face turned up towards his questioningly.

'What can I bet my life about?'

'That there's a good time coming,' said the Sergeant, with more of his highly unofficial treatment. 'What do you guess, now — a clever girl like you?'

'As if I possibly could!'

The Sergeant looked down on her with immense satisfaction. And indeed in a rather unobvious way she was pretty enough to gladden any eyes. But she had to be looked twice at. Hers was a beauty of the second sight. It seemed a queer fate which had made a policewoman of her.

'Try,' urged the Sergeant. 'Think what it is we've all been needing in this station?'

'Something to do?' she suggested.

'You never spoke a truer word. And what do you think we've got?'

She raised her eyebrows.

'A murder!' he said thrillingly. 'A

murder — up at Harrington Convent —'

'Not — by one of the nuns?'

'By one of the ladies!' The Sergeant looked shocked. 'What a question! Why, I thought you liked nuns.'

'So I do. Though they scare me rather. What goes on inside their heads?'

'Ah, you may ask. That's what a many would like to know. No, it ain't by a nun, nor yet of a nun, but it's a murder all the same. And do you mean to tell me — a clever girl like you — as you can't see anything for yourself in a start like this?'

'For me? A bit of stooging, perhaps —'

'You want a good smack. Stoogin' indeed! Listen now to what's come into your uncle's head —'

And he whispered.

Olive, it should be said, was almost the daughter by adoption of Sergeant Baseldon and his 'Missus'. It was ten thousand pities that this excellent couple, with a world of love to bestow, should be childless; but, finding that Olive was an orphan, and entirely without friends in Harrington — if indeed she had any anywhere — they had adopted her, and

14

were never so happy as when she was about the house. They treated her, and fussed about her, exactly as if she were their own child. Her tendency to disabling 'moods', for instance — intervals of some mysterious unhappiness which came over the girl from time to time — how they had discussed these together, the 'Missus' suspecting a 'fellow' in the background, the Sergeant — who could not abide the thought of a 'fellow' — blaming her loneliness and the austerity of the police life.

Olive laughed when the Sergeant had done whispering, and shook her head.

'Not a hope. Besides, I told you, nuns scare me. And the Super would never —'

'You leave the Super to me. And what do you want to be scared of nuns for, you silly girl?'

'Of course I'm not really *scared*. But they come into my dreams sometimes — with those crosses they wear —'

'A baby, that's what you are. A convent job! Why, it might have been arranged to suit you. The ladies'll feel it a delicacy in us sendin' 'em a nice clever girl like you as they can be free with. Now, just you wait here while I go in to the Super —'

He was gone a very short time, and returned beaming.

'What did I tell you? Super thinks it a brainy idea; says, if you handle it smart, it'll be the making of you. I'm to go with you. Lordy, but won't I be proud bein' bossed about by you. Off with you now, and make yourself look the way you know how. I want the Ladies to see what kind of a girl you are.'

'More to the point if they knew what kind of a man *you* are,' Olive said. And she went and did her best to please him, excitement upon her and a strange sense as of the fulfilment of prophecy.

Nuns! What sort of people were they *really*?

Nuns —

'Ready, Chief?' came a hail from the Sergeant.

'Chief' indeed! But what a darling he was!

Some fifteen minutes later a small, rather anomalous group of persons presented itself humbly at the back

16

regions of the Convent and was greeted there by Mother Assistant.

3

Verity Acquaints Herself with the Facts

'What's all this rot?'

So said Miss Verity Goodchild as, swaying gracefully, she read Mother Peagle's notice over the nondescript heads of numerous Middle Schoolers — some of which she lightly cuffed much as a bishop at Confirmation lightly cuffs a candidate on the cheek to remind him or her of those buffets of the world which he or she may confidently expect.

The nondescripts wriggled but made no reply. They were all in great awe of Verity, who, though not a Ribbon, was away up at the dizzy top of the School, and a dark and secret power.

Verity suppressed a sigh. Life was a bit dull now that all her contemporaries, even Philomene Watts and the feather-brained Jamette Kestrel, were Ribbons. She did not envy them or grudge their promotion, but she did miss those former selves in them which the magisterial Ribbon had affected, in her opinion, for the worse.

She re-read the notice, deliberately occupying about three times as much space as she needed so as to mortify the curiosity of her juniors and teach them that 'Life is real and life is earnest.'

'A case in point,' she remarked to herself. 'Now if the Peaglums had made a Ribbon of *me* when she jolly well ought, it would be my painful duty not only to keep all these little donkeys out of the kitchen-gardens but also to keep out myself. As things are, however — ' And, pushing aside the scrum of supernumeraries, she passed out with studied negligence through the cloister door into the garden. No-body saw her as, with a quick glance around, she slipped in among the bushes *en route* for the forbidden ground.

'This ought to be a lesson to the Peaglums. She is quite old enough to know that you cannot have things both ways.'

Verity had indeed ever been an

independent thinker. That was why she was not a Ribbon. Independent thinkers do not become Blue Ribbons or Cabinet Ministers.

Verity was now seventeen. She had matured. She was — not engaged to, but had a profound understanding with that Mr. 'Johnny' Guest of the *Peephole* newspaper, who had perceived in her at a fevered glance an 'helpmeet' unto his many-sided life. She met him in town at least twice every holidays, with a broadening effect on her mind. There was no secret about this; Major and Mrs. Goodchild knew as much about it as they were capable of knowing about their daughter's proceedings. Verity, under the influence of Mr. Guest, proposed a meantime career of journalism spiced with crime-detection when she left school.

Such a girl as Verity, left without the steadying power of responsibility at so crucial a time in her life, might have been a bad influence. It may be doubted if leaving Verity without a Ribbon was Mother Peagle at her brightest and best.

But prejudice dies hard, and nowhere so hard as in really conscientious schoolmistresses. As a matter of fact, Verity was not a bad influence — or a good one; she was simply indifferent.

And so it was that, in spite of recent injunction, here was Verity presently wriggling a rather puerile passage through the shrubberies to the kitchen-gardens.

She was a born sleuth. There was not a trick of the trade she had not grasped. She had an eye, intuition and, that mysterious thing, luck. Luck certainly seems to stand by those who generously trust in it, and Verity generously trusted in her luck. As she surveyed the considerable area of the kitchen-gardens, and she without a notion of what to look for, luck directed her eye to the rubbish-dump.

Nobody was about. The scene was unaltered since Mr. Turtle quitted it. The body lay where it had been found, covered partly with its original brown paper and partly with some sacking thrown over it by Mr. Turtle. One feature of it was, however, plainly visible in spite of brown paper and sacking.

A foot stuck out.

Verity's soul cried out within her.

'I do believe —! It can't be —! But —'

Any feelings of distaste she might have had were overwhelmed by excitement.

'A body! Another body! Oh, what *fun*!'

Perhaps Mother Peagle was right. Ribbons should be nice-minded girls, shrinking properly away from the macabre in all its forms and not exclaiming 'What fun!' of a corpse on a dump. But Verity was not seeing a corpse on a dump, she was seeing that most living and beautiful thing, scope. Scope — opportunity — call it what you please. She was seeing what Olive Churston was to see later. She was seeing what 'stout Cortez' saw from his 'peak in Darien'. She was seeing what all the fuss of the French Revolution was about — *la carrière ouverte aux talents*.

But excitement did not deprive her of prudence. She approached as near as she could to the dump but never so as to leave cover. She kept an eye open for Mr. Turtle, and the other for the spritely ubiquity of Juan Copanza. She kept both ears alert for sounds of the approaching police. She knew better than to touch or tamper with anything. But from the nearest point she could reach she observed the protruding foot with intensity, and was soon deducing away like Sherlock Holmes himself. It is the Watsons of this world who suppose that all feet are much of a muchness, the Sherlocks and the Veritys know that from one foot you can deduce the whole body of which it is part.

Thus Verity decided at once that it was not an English foot.

This was no pavement foot. It had gone bare as often as shod, and over rough country too. The sole was toughened, the toes uncrushed, the nails perfect. Verity had been out in Malta when her father was stationed there, and she had noted the large, capable, wholesome feet of the peasants. This was a foot not unlike — a peasant foot. There are no peasants in England today.

Verity had another brainwave, though at first it would not come. Ah, she had it.

The *position* of the body — on a rubbish-dump — thrown there presumably by the murderer — what would Sherlock make of that? Elementary, my dear Watson. Why, scorn! Scorn — contempt — and contumely.

A peasant murdered and thrown in scorn on a rubbish-dump!

Watson would shrug helpless shoulders, but Sherlock, knowing what foreigners are, would be on to it at once —

Politics!

All foreigners are mixed up in politics: this man was a foreigner: *ergo* —

And, mind you, politics are no fun in foreign countries. Now, presently, what politics are the most dangerous? Even Watson could hardly have failed here.

'A Communist! A 'liquidated' Communist —'

It was at this point of triumphant deduction that Verity was admonished by that sixth sense which she possessed in common with all great detectives — indeed, with all great minds. Her thumbs pricked, and she knew it was time to go.

She sighed. She had been getting on so

well, but now she must give way to the more cumbrous mental processes of the official. Nor could she hope to be able to resume, for the body would now become the property of the police, always so jealous of amateur aid. Moreover, if she stayed any longer she might have to account for her lateness to that brilliant Wrangler of Cambridge, Mother Bracken, who presided over Senior Mathematics at Harrington.

With a last long look at that foot which had told her so much Verity began her retreat, sustained by the thought that the Ribbons would be just emerging from their solemn pow-wow with the Peaglums, and it would be fun to gloat privately over their foolish young faces.

But then, suddenly, she stiffened and fell flat down on the ground in the covert where she was.

Something was moving ahead of her.

Was it Copanza? No, it was not. But it had come from the hut where Copanza lived. It was scared, and preserving as much caution as Verity herself.

'I may not be a Ribbon, but —' Verity

told herself; and by a series of masterly movements she outmanœuvred the fugitive, which, finding itself waylaid, sank down in a huddle, covering its face with its hands.

Verity, picking it up and standing it on its feet, found herself confronting — Inez Escapado.

'Inez. Whatever do you think you're doing?'

'What busyness is it of yours? You are not a R-r-ibbon, so I t'ink. What do *you* t'ink you do? If you tell of me, Verity Goodchild, I also shall tell of you.'

'What's the matter with you?' Verity inquired in a tone of real sympathy and concern, for Inez was obviously keyed up to some very high pitch indeed.

'Nuzzing. Only I am not able to find where — Juan is. Do you know where Juan is?'

Verity shook her head. 'I haven't seen him. And look here, Inez, don't do this again. I may not be a Ribbon, but I'm older than you, and I can tell you things are pretty serious, and it won't do Juan any good to have you running after him.'

'I do not know what to do,' Inez said in a despairing voice, speaking, it seemed, to herself rather than to Verity.

'You're — afraid of something,' Verity said.

'Yes, yes. I am afraid —'

'Then you'd better tell me. Not now; we haven't time, but as soon as you can. I might be able to help. I will if I can. You look to me as if you ought to go to the infirmary —'

'No. I must find where Juan is. You do not understand. Oh, it is terrible — terrible —'

'It probably isn't as bad as you think, you poor kid,' Verity said, feeling ages older than the shuddering girl at her side. 'Come, we must get back in school now. But, Inez —'

'Oh, what —?'

'I tell you what I'd do if it was me, and the thing was serious —'

'Serious? Yes, it is serious. What would you do, Verity?'

'I'd spill the whole bally tin of beans right out to Reverend Mother.'

'Ze — beans? Oh yes, I understand.

Reverend Muzzer? Oh, but I can never do that. She will not even believe me —'

'If it's real, she will.'

'God knows it is real —'

'Well, that's something to hold on to — that God knows. Inez, I do want to help. I'm giving you the best advice I know. Reverend Mother *will* believe. And she'll be able to help. Do now, like a good kid. I don't care what it is — battle, murder or sudden death — Reverend Mother will be able to help.'

'Verity. There is battle — there is murder — I t'ink dere will be sudden death — for me — soon, quick, now — unless something become. It is not dat Reverend Muzzer *will* not to understand — she is unable — she cannot —'

'Don't you believe it. Do as I tell you. Stick up your chin, and remember you're the daughter of the Hazh Bazh.'

'Oh, Verity, I t'ink my fazzer is dead — and my muzzer — and all my family right down to de last little baby — to Grandissimo Superbo —'

'Well, I think they aren't. You poor little thing. Promise me, Inez — don't put it off

— go today and tell Reverend Mother.'

'I t'ink,' Inez murmured, 'perhaps I must —'

4

A Parliament of Ribbons

No trace of recent guilt or strong emotion remained on Verity's fresh-coloured and incorrigibly cheerful face when she got back into school in nice time to see the Ribbons emerging from the conference with Mother Peagle.

She waited to make sure that their eyes were upon her, and then went and stood among a group of very junior juniors, where she performed an act of holding the Ribbons in awe if not terror.

The Ribbons as usual looked uncomfortable, except, of course, Torquilla and the black-avised Alauda Gale, who remarked:

'That one is getting a bit stale, Verity. Not so funny as it was.'

Verity suddenly decided to forgive the Ribbons, for the moment anyhow.

'Sorry, Alauda. I'll try to think up

something quite new. There's nothing I wouldn't do for a Ribbon.' She added:

'How's the Peaglums this morning? Why this sudden prejudice against the kitchen-gardens? What's the Great Secret?'

Alauda (the Hon. Alauda Gale) merely smiled an aggravating smile down the sides of her undoubtedly Norman nose. It was the slender Philomene, always concerned for Verity, who replied.

'*Is* there a secret?'

'Don't be disingenuous,' Verity reproved. 'This Ribbon racket is corrupting you, Phil. Where is your pristine candour?'

'Where is her — *what*?' It was the mighty Torquilla, Head of the School, who demanded. 'What words you do use, Verity! You really are a prize ass.'

'It's *second* prize while you're about.' And Verity dodged the cuff which Torquilla aimed at her head.

By what seemed strange coincidence — or perhaps it was the workings of an interior grace — all the Ribbons had gathered round, so that Verity stood like Joseph among the brethren.

'Why this sudden affection?' she asked.

'It isn't,' Alauda replied. 'It's scientific interest.'

And there was a general smirk.

This was annoying. It was one thing for Verity to have secrets apart from the Ribbons, quite another for the Ribbons to have a secret apart from her. The creatures obviously *had* a secret.

They had. Little as Verity knew it, the chief subject of discussion at the recent conference had been — Verity herself.

Mother Peagle had opened the proceedings by stressing the importance of the ban on the kitchen-gardens, but, quick at the uptake, she had noted a certain lack of response, not to say glumness, on the faces around her. She had paused accordingly, waiting for the glumness to find expression.

Torquilla spoke.

'I bet you anything you like, Mother —'

But Mother Peagle had gone stone deaf, as she always did when a manner of speech distressed her.

Torquilla tried again.

'Of course we'll take care about the kitchen-gardens, Mother, but —'

'Yes, Torquilla?'

'Well — I shouldn't be at all surprised if Verity was having a good nose round there at this minute —'

'A good — *what*, Torquilla?'

'Well, a good *look* round.'

'Come, Torquilla. Verity must have seen the notice —'

'Yes. But, Mother —'

It was Philomene speaking, and actually interrupting. But a change had been coming over Philomene of late: still as slender, as fragile, as heartbreakingly pretty, she was beginning to show a strong practical side. Mother Peagle, whose wisdom had not failed her with Philomene as it had with Verity, rejoiced, and was always glad to hear Philomene's voice raised in council.

'Yes, Philomene?'

'You see, Mother — though Verity pretends, she doesn't like not being a Ribbon. I think she feels — at her age —'

Mother Peagle suppressed a sigh: the problem of Verity, a girl she loved and therefore chastened, was always on her conscience.

'I fear Verity is as irresponsible as ever,' she answered Philomene.

'No, Mother. Excuse me, but really she isn't. You know how Verity pretends. But she *is* seventeen, and at seventeen you can't help being responsible. You just *feel* it, and that's all about it. If Verity still behaves funnily, it's because her position is so funny — so senior, such a born leader, and yet not a Ribbon. It's awfully hard on Verity, Mother —'

There was a chorus of agreement — loudest perhaps in Alauda Gale, that shrewd and pugnacious young person, who on the whole did not like Verity, and had certainly less affection than the others for Mother Peagle.

'Yes, Alauda?'

'I think Philomene is right. It's a nuisance Verity's not being a Ribbon. It would make things a lot easier for *us* if she was.'

'Does she — obstruct you?'

'Oh dear, no. Nothing so obvious. She just — sort of — *grins* at us —'

'Smiles —?'

'No, Mother: *grins!*'

Another chorus of approval, above which the voice of Philomene was again heard.

'I do wish you would think about it, Mother. You always decide right. Nothing can stop a person like Verity from being an influence. I'm sure it would be for the good of the School if she were a Ribbon.'

'You, Torquilla?' said Mother Peagle.

'I'm all for it, Mother. Verity wasn't any more of a little beast than the rest of us, but she somehow, without meaning to, drew more attention to herself. She got people's goat —'

'*What* did she do?'

'I don't know how else to put it, Mother. I mean, Verity did things in a special way. It was partly that nose of hers —'

There was an outburst of laughter, to which even Mother Peagle was forced to contribute a smile. Verity's nose had a unique slight tilt which put it out of her power to look anything but cheerful, even under reprimand, even in chapel on Good Friday.

Ribbon feeling, it appeared, ran strongly in Verity's favour. Such opposition as there was came from Prudence Rockingham, who held, and always had done, that because she was virtuous there ought to be no more 'cakes and ale'.

'Yes, Prudence?'

'I am sorry to disagree with Torquilla and Philomene, Mother, but I must say what I think or fail in my duty. I hope I have no uncharitable feelings —'

'Oh bother!' — *sotto voce* but general.

' — but when I look back I cannot help seeing how often I myself had to regret the influence of Verity. She was, of course, younger then, but I see nothing in her today which makes me think she is more serious and conscientious.'

'Utter nonsense! If you mean she isn't a general wet-blanket like you —'

'Hush, Philomene.' And Mother Peagle again looked towards Torquilla.

'Well, Mother, I can look back as far as Prudence — and so can Phil and Alauda

— and all I can say is *I* never regretted Verity's influence.'

'Would I have been her best friend?' burst out Philomene.

'What have you younger Ribbons got to say?' inquired Mother Peagle.

A certain Muriel Maitland answered — a quietly forceful girl, not unlikely to be Head of the School next year.

'We feel very awkward about Verity, Mother. I think most of us like her very much. Certainly I do. I don't believe she was ever a bad influence, and I'm sure she would be a good one now.'

'Good,' said Torquilla: which was exactly the length at which she liked to deliver herself.

'I shall certainly not overlook a point on which so many of you are agreed,' said Mother Peagle. 'I am most heartily with you in liking Verity for herself —'

'Oh, Mother, do make Verity a Ribbon.' It was Philomene, again interrupting.

'Hush,' admonished Prudence.

'Oh, you shut up —'

' — and in thinking,' went on Mother Peagle, 'that her cheerfulness would be an asset to us. I shall earnestly reconsider the matter. Remember, Philomene, only the grace of God can bring us to right judgments.'

'Yes, Mother, but please do make Verity a Ribbon —'

The meeting then broke up.

Well might Verity suspect a secret.

5

Mr. Turtle Meets his Match

There is a belief very current in this world of errors that nuns are 'old-fashioned' people, easily shocked and opposed to 'progress' in all its forms.

Olive did not find this in Mother Assistant. Even the venerable lay-sister who mounted guard over the back door only smiled a weirdly omniscient smile when told that a young woman was in charge of the police party.

All the 'shock' indeed was on the other side. 'Assistant!' inwardly exclaimed Sergeant Baseldon when the truth of the field-officer dawned on him. 'I'd like to see the woman as that one is *assistant* to!'

'Why, she's only a girl,' thought Mother Assistant as she stole glances at Olive. She was astonished but not in the least shocked by the phenomenon of a young woman armed with the authority of the law.

'I am so glad to meet you, Miss — Churston. I am Reverend Mother's assistant, and she thought it might be a help if I went round with you and explained things a bit. But please say if you would rather go alone.'

'I would much rather you came. But — it's sometimes not very nice, you know. I mean —'

'Oh, I've been a V.A.D. in my time, and all sorts of things. It would interest me to see how you set about an affair like this —'

'And so you are really a nun,' Olive said, with a frank look, as they set off.

Mother Assistant laughed.

'Am I as bad as you expected?'

'I am not quite sure what I did expect,' Olive said, 'but not — not like you.'

She flushed, not feeling quite sure if this was polite. She had a very pretty flush.

Mother Assistant thought so.

'And you are not at all my idea of a lady detective.'

'Thank goodness for that!' Olive said.

And they both laughed.

Verity, seated aloft at a front window paying but little heed to what she described as the 'unspeakable gibberish' pouring from the lips of Mother Bracken, saw the police party pass by, recognized it for what it was, and almost fell out with excitement.

'I do believe it's a girl 'tec. They have them now. Johnny told me. Oh, how I wish it was me! How glorious to be her!'

Fortunately Mother Bracken was too much absorbed in her positively astral theorem to take notice, but the Ribbons took notice, and were furious with Verity for risking a conduct mark at a time when Mother Peagle might be actually on her knees in that 'earnest reconsideration' which she had promised.

How just like Verity!

Mother Assistant felt definitely nervous for her new favourite, as, on approaching the dump, they found Mr. Turtle standing beside it, obviously in what Reverend Mother called one of his 'impossible' humours. Mr. Turtle seemed always to have a presentiment of a crisis, and to stop shaving in due time ahead.

'I am afraid our man is sometimes a little — difficult,' she whispered to Olive.

But Olive was young and believed that Turtles are only a matter of handling.

'Good morning, Mr. Turtle. How horrid for you this morning. So this is your dump. What a beauty! I should like to have a look over it when I've asked you a few questions.'

However it may be with nuns, with Mr. Turtle it was certainly true that he was old-fashioned, easily shocked and opposed to progress in all its forms. He was not aware that such creatures as Olive existed. He hated being 'spoke pert to by a young gal'. He gave Olive a look all over (at which the Sergeant bristled), and he spat aside.

'And 'oo may you be, if a man may ast a plain question?'

'My name is Churston,' Olive answered pleasantly. 'I am a police officer, and at present looking into this case.'

'You're a — wot? Say them words again, will yer?'

'No. Once is quite enough. Begin now and give your evidence —'

'I'll see you in 'ell — a — a cheesemite like you!'

'Do you give this man in charge for obstruction and insultin' be'aviour, Miss Olive?' said the Sergeant.

'No. I'll cope with him.'

'You'll cope with him, will yer? I'll wring your little weasand —'

'Now look here, Turnip — or whatever your name is —' Police-Surgeon Goodall was beginning.

Olive interrupted. 'Excuse me, Doctor —' And she faced Mr. Turtle, who was working himself up into a kind of hornpipe or Highland fling of rage.

'Don't be so silly. You've no idea what a fool you look. Listen to me. You have been told what I am, and you know you must obey the law. You will do as I tell you or I shall have you locked up until you do. Another insult, more of that ridiculous behaviour, and off you go.'

At this the Sergeant and a policeman moved over and stood one at each side of

Mr. Turtle, ready at a word from Olive to 'run him in'.

Mother Assistant had never expected to see such a day.

There ensued a sort of staggered instant, during which foreknowledge itself was at a loss what to foreknow — and Mr. Turtle did as he was told.

His evidence was a sorry performance considered as Turtle, and he looked the grief and humiliation in which he was plunged. He could not understand why his natural objection to the authority of a chit of a girl, himself nearing seventy, should have involved him in disaster. Perhaps the world was getting too much for Mr. Turtle, the 'hungry generations' treading him down.

When he had — not come to one of his usual perorations but simply 'dried up', Olive asked him a few questions.

'You have a help, I understand — a young Spaniard, name of Copanza?'

'Which 'e is not a 'elp but a 'indrance.'

'That will do. What I want to know is, have you seen the young man this morning — since the discovery of the body?'

'I 'ave not.'

'He lives on the premises? In that hut over there, doesn't he? Have you been to look for him?'

'Why should I?'

'Will you please answer my question. Have you looked for him?'

'I 'ave not, nor I wouldn't demean myself.'

'It hasn't struck you as odd that he is not about?'

'Why should it?'

'Will you not ask me questions but answer mine. Can you suggest a reason why this man should not be at work as usual?'

'I cannot. And reason why. 'Cos I never give 'im a thought.'

'Please do so now. Do you know where he is?'

'I do' know nothink about him. Nor I do' want to know nothink about him.'

'You are a very unsatisfactory witness.' And Olive turned away from Mr. Turtle, on her heel, so to speak, dropping him as if he were some failure in his own vegetable world, and spoke to the Sergeant.

'We must account for this man. Will you go over and search the hut, Sergeant? See if it shows any signs of sudden departure. Have a look in the bushes too; he may be scared and hiding.'

Next minute she was supervising a photographer and his work, giving expert directions and using the jargon of photography, to Mother Assistant's edification. The body was meanwhile moved into an empty greenhouse, where Dr. Goodall followed it like a scientific vulture. He had the air of one saying to himself, 'I'll larn you to be a dead body!' and he did most thoroughly 'larn' it.

Olive assisted him, and seemed in her quickly assumed surgical head-dress and gloves as much at home in autopsy as in photography.

'However did she pick it all up? How old can she be?' Mother Assistant was thinking as, moved by old V.A.D. memories, she watched the grisly proceedings through the glass.

After a deal of general poking and probing Dr. Goodall seemed to pounce. There was a little quick work with scalpel and forceps, a grunt from the man of science, and the latter instrument was withdrawn tightly locked upon some small object, which he showed to Olive, remarking facetiously, 'Here's what done it, ma'am. Shot at dam' short range — through the kidneys — with these little jokers!'

Olive nodded, and immediately went outside to receive the report of the Sergeant, just returned from the hut.

The Sergeant had drawn a complete blank. The door of the hut was not locked, everything within was orderly, there were no 'firearms or other lethal weapons', nothing was suspicious, and nothing offered a hint as to the present whereabouts of the wanted man.

'My own belief is, miss, he'll be coming back to that hut, with a headache.'

Olive's composure had been perfect through-out the proceedings, but now she began to look exhausted, and there was a trace of exasperation in her manner. She frowned for a moment as if in deep thought, and then turned to Mother Assistant.

'You probably know all about that hut — er — madam. Has it a cellar or storehouse underneath — anywhere for a man to hide in?'

'No, Miss Churston. I was present myself when it was erected. It is just a little one-room pre-fab. There is only insulation under the floor. To my certain knowledge no cellar or store-house.'

But Olive, still frowning, was straining her eyes across at the hut.

'What's all that *digging* round the place?' she asked in a general way.

'They been growing celery there, miss, or so I'd think,' said the Sergeant.

Mother Assistant nodded confirmation.

But at this moment there was a diversion. A small police-van much like a coffin on wheels had sidled into position. There was considerable shuffling of large feet as all officers joined in consigning the draped corpse within. Mother Assistant reverently knelt, and Olive, after a glance, did likewise. The van drove away with its burden to some place of mortuary where it would await identification. Noses were generally blown. The bleak and godless little ceremony was at an end.

'Dingy, isn't it?' Olive was saying to Mother Assistant. 'They always leave out this part in the crime stories.'

'You — you feel the lack of religion?' Mother Assistant gently suggested. 'Yes, it is godlessness which exhausts.'

Mother Assistant was not a shining light or a person of penetrating intelligence, but one thing she did know when she saw it, and that was a tired girl.

'Miss Churston,' she went on, 'I know you are very busy, but I wish I could persuade you to come in with me for a cup of tea or coffee. You really need it. You could tell us how best we can help the police. And then there is Reverend Mother — she would be so much interested to meet you.'

'Very kind of her — of you,' Olive said, obviously striving not to be brusque; 'but I am afraid not just now — with this wretched man on my mind. And I can't just butt in on you —'

'Go and do what the lady says,' muttered the Sergeant in the background.

'I am not in the least tired,' Olive

flashed, thus proving the contrary.

It is only by constant small charities and courtesies that a community life can be maintained, and the care of children and the younger members calls for affectionate manners and modes of speech; and so Mother Assistant was easily able to make nothing of Olive's unwillingness, to persist against it, to indulge it and yet exert authority.

'My dear, you will not be 'butting in'. Come, now.' And she gently took Olive's arm.

'Go and do what the lady says,' muttered the Sergeant.

Olive yielded. Perhaps with not the very best grace, but she yielded, and permitted herself to be led at a gentle pace back into the main gardens and up over soft turf to the beautiful Georgian façade of the Convent with its pillars, great windows and low steps.

'How pretty it is!' Olive exclaimed. And already her voice sounded rested.

As they entered, an interior door was heard to open, almost as if it were cause and effect, and the slight figure of a nun was seen approaching — a figure of the most immediate power and winning charm. She walked fast, and smoothly as though upon the water. An interior warmth filled Olive, and gone from her heart was that disconsolate sense, that sense of something lacking, which was somewhere at the base of her life. For this woman brought with her, shining in her eyes and informing her whole body, a radiant reassurance — a very 'substance of things hoped for, an evidence of things unseen'.

'Miss Churston. My dear, how very good of you to spare me a few minutes. Come in here at once, where you can rest.'

And she put a strangely alive arm round Olive, drawing her in.

'Reverend Mother —' murmured Mother Assistant.

But this Olive definitely did not need to be told.

6

Reverend Mother Reads
The Times Newspaper

At a fixed hour every day Reverend Mother was in the habit of quickly and expertly scanning through *The Times*.

This is not to be taken as a sidelight on her character but on the position she held as head of a cosmopolitan institution.

Harrington was such an institution: its human complement included, among choir-nuns, lay-sisters and children, many not entitled to the blessing of a British passport.

It thus behoved Reverend Mother to keep abreast of foreign politics. Therefore she read *The Times*.

This, and a confidential friend at the Foreign Office, kept her reasonably well informed as to the main tendencies of events in even the most obscure countries.

Only a few days before the discovery of the body on the dump her eye had been caught, her attention fixed, by about an eighth of a column to the following effect:

'News from Anaconda continues to be conflicting — according to its source. It seems, however, to be established that the Communist rising against the Hazh Bazh, Don Magnifiguo Escapado, far from having been repressed, has been successful in capturing the capital city of Lilitha and in forcing the Hazh Bazh and his adherents into the jungle. The legation emphatically denies the rumour from a Communist source that he and his entire family have been put to death. While undoubtedly a dubious situation exists in Anaconda there is reason to believe that Don Magnifiguo still constitutes the dominating factor. He is a master of jungle warfare.'

'I should not be at all surprised,' Reverend Mother commented to herself;

and, completing her perusal of the paper, and folding it neatly, she rang up her friend — one Sir Clement de Willowby — at the Foreign Office.

'Anaconda?' said the cheerful voice of Sir Clement. 'If I were you I shouldn't worry at all, Reverend Mother. If I know anything about Escapado, he isn't done for yet — not by a long chalk. I'll let you have any lowdown there is. No trouble at all. Delighted. Best love to Senorita Inez.'

Reverend Mother then sent for Inez. It was her custom to have a private word or two from time to time with all the foreign children, and so there was nothing out of the way in her doing this.

'Well, Inez, my child —'

The lapse of two years had taken nothing from the exotic beauty of Inez but rather added to it. At fourteen she was exquisite. If she was less now the perfect little savage which had once thrilled Reverend Mother's imagination, there was a new depth to her, a greater warmth and glow, which thrilled Reverend Mother even more. There were nothing but good reports of her, for she was the soul of prudence in all things. The only people to find her a little trying sometimes were her classmates and the Ribbons, because of a certain patronage which showed in her manner to both. She felt older than English fourteen-year-olds, and she could not understand what such great creatures as Torquilla, say, were doing still at school when by Anacondan standards they ought to be married and the mothers of at least one child.

'Dear Reverend Muzzer —'

Reverend Mother did not come straight to her point but kept the talk general for a while, satisfying herself from the girl's natural manner that she was in no present alarm.

It was after some time that she said:

'And how are all your people in Anaconda, Inez? Is your brother Jacquimo as good a correspondent as ever?'

'Oh yes, t'ank you, Reverend Muzzer, all my family are ver' well — from my great-grandfazzer down to de little baby-brother, Grandissimo Superbo. I have long letter from Jacquee five, six days ago. He say it is ver' amusing in

Lilitha just now because of de Communists dat shoot at us always and say dey will throw us all to de crocodiles.'

'He finds that amusing, does he?' said Reverend Mother. 'I have always wanted to meet Jacquimo.'

'Perhaps he come to England someday to see me. He has great curiosity to see England because of de funny t'ings which I write him about de English.'

Reverend Mother could only wonder what sort of figure the Community cut in these pages.

'You are not nervous, Inez — about the Communists?'

Inez shrugged. 'Oh no, Reverend Muzzer. Jacquee tell me it is all O.K. It is not ver' easy to kill my fazzer. Many people try. Most days. But,' with a gesture, 'he is not dead.'

'Are you sorry to be away from Anaconda at this 'amusing' time, Inez?'

'I regret sometimes, Reverend Muzzer. But I am obedient to my fazzer. In Anaconda a daughter is obedient to her fazzer. My fazzer say, Anaconda is bad, bad, bad, but dat is one of de good t'ings, dat de childrens obeys their parents. Besides, Reverend Muzzer,' Inez went on, 'even in England, among all your policemen and with your English Constitution, I share in the dangers of my family.'

'Surely not, Inez.'

'Oh, but yes, Reverend Muzzer. If de Communists wish to kill *all* of us, dey will not miss me out. Dey will send a *bazh* — I beg your pardon, a man — to kill me also. In de Convent here, wiz all de big windows, it is easy for someone to climb in and kill me.'

Good God!

Inez did not hear this inward exclamation of Reverend Mother's. She did not see any outward sign of it on the perfectly controlled face. All she knew was that after a short silence Reverend Mother put an arm round her, drawing her closer to her side.

When Reverend Mother spoke, it was beside the point.

'What do you think your father meant, Inez, when he said Anaconda was bad, bad, bad?'

'He mean that in Anaconda dere are no laws and parliaments and — and t'ings — '

'Does he think there ought to be?'

'Oh yes. He say to me, if ever he can settle with dese Communists he will make laws and have parliaments, and teach de people not to kill so much, and not throw anybody to de crocodiles. He was beginning to try to do some of dese t'ings, but de people only t'ink he is not so strong as he was, so they listen to de Communists, who tell zem dat a man of their own, a man called Marx, ought to be de Hazh Bazh.'

'Yes,' Reverend Mother said. 'I am very sorry for your father. The most difficult thing in the world is to teach people to have new and better ideas.' She broke off, and went on, still holding the girl close to her.

'I think we shall have to hide you at night for a little while. Not because I fear anything but because it is wise to take every precaution.'

'Dey will find me, Reverend Muzzer, if dey come. Yet it is right to take precautions. My fazzer is ver' brave, ver' clever man, but never forget precaution.'

Reverend Mother got up and went to a large cupboard, out of which she produced some object. It glittered, and so did Inez's eyes when she saw it.

'Do you remember the trouble I had to get you to part with this when you first came to us?' Reverend Mother said. 'Now I think it right to give it back to you. Don't let anyone see it, and don't on any account use it unless —'

Inez nodded.

'I have learned English manners now, Reverend Muzzer. Still, I am ver' glad to have 'im back.'

And the object, which was a small dagger, vanished adroitly under her school-frock.

Reverend Mother had been as good as her word, and Inez slept in a number of hide-outs, never without a nun hard by.

The watchful nun had sometimes been Reverend Mother herself.

But then had come the mystery of the dead man on the dump and the disappearance of Juan Copanza.

Inez had that very day gone into the infirmary with what seemed some sort of hysterical breakdown. Mother Infirmarian issued sad reports of her condition. The doctor had come, given a soothing injection, advised absolute quiet —

But Inez could not be quiet. She kept forever starting up in bed declaring with wild eyes that the garden was full of deadly snakes. She cried out for 'Juan — Juan', but more often for somebody called 'Diego' — whom nobody knew.

The doctor came again and stayed a long while, watching Inez closely.

He interviewed Reverend Mother.

'Do you know of anything she may have on her mind?'

Reverend Mother gave him a very guarded account of things which might well be on Inez's mind.

The doctor pulled a long face and promised to come again first thing in the morning.

Reverend Mother made up her mind. She consulted no one. She was the last woman to cry out for help but the first to realize when help must at all costs be had.

Effective help.

'I shall let Mr. Pearson at least *hear* about this.'

7

Told in Gath

But the schemes even of Reverend Mothers 'gang aft agley'.

Murder will out, and the secret of the dead body could not be kept from the School.

Ask not how it leaked out. The Ribbons did their best. Verity disclosed nothing. Mr. Turtle, still suffering from aggravated shock, was silent.

None the less, the secret leaked out in the School, and, what was far worse, it became known to the parents.

Now parents are, and rightly are, the great terror of all school authorities. They care nothing for policy. They cannot see the whole wood but only the one particular tree of their own planting. They are indifferent to the 'greatest good of the greatest number'. How is Polly affected? How is John? That is, and forever will be, the war-cry of the parents.

Harrington Lane — still a 'lane' in respect of narrowness and blind bends — is, of course, a chosen speeding-ground for motorists; and to the ordinarily lethal nature of the traffic there was added now a constant stream of light-hearted lads on red motor-cycles who rode as though they were bringing the Good News from Ghent to Aix. One such would hand in a cable from the Lady Gale at Bordighera asking if it was really safe for the Honourable Alauda to stay at Harrington? Now, Alauda was no chicken; she was seventeen, a Ribbon, and about the toughest girl in the School.

More excusable was the anxiety of the MacBinkie of MacBinkie for his Thistle, a harebell of a child. But it was a pity that his strong Scottish nationalist principles compelled him to wire in Gaelic. The boy had to be kept waiting until a certain Mother McVehoy, who alone knew Gaelic, could be run down in some remote sphere of usefulness and asked what it was exactly the MacBinkie wished to be reassured about.

Reverend Mother's post-bag swelled out to mammoth proportions, for not only did almost every parent want advice by return but all generations of 'Old Children' birographed endless pages of sympathy and begged for 'just a line when you are not too busy'.

There was also the Press. Whatever happens in a convent (except the prayer) is 'news', and the public must have it. But here Harrington was provided: a certain Mother Gogg, who had heard the 'still, small voice' of vocation above the roar of printing machines in Fleet Street, handled the needs of the Press to perfection, and enjoyed herself into the bargain.

The great thing was, of course, to prevent such a boiling over of parental solicitude as to cause a general descent upon Harrington. This was successfully done — except in the instance of the Lady Gale, who jet-planed from Bordighera; of old Admiral Hercules, who was as deaf as a post but had three little granddaughters at the School; of Mr. and

Mrs. Smith, who always arrive every-where in any sort of a crisis; and some dozen or so others.

The telephone went without stopping.

Reverend Mother rang up Mr. Pearson at the Yard.

'Is that Scotland Yard? Good evening. This is Reverend Mother of Harrington Convent. Can I speak to Chief-Inspector Pearson, please?'

'Hold on, madam. I will put you through to the Deputy Commissioner —'

'Oh, but I don't want — ' Reverend Mother was beginning; but the receiver gargled at her, and she realized that whether she wanted the Deputy Commissioner or no she had got to have him.

Nuisances, these telephones! And yet — what a blessing!

'Reverend Mother —' the telephone mildly exclaimed in accents unmistakably Mr. Pearson's.

Oh, thank God he was not away on a case!

'Good evening to you, Mr. Pearson. But what is all this? They insisted on putting me through to the Deputy

Commissioner —'

'Very much at your service,' murmured the voice.

'Do you mean — *you* are the Deputy?'

The voice deprecated assent.

'You the Deputy! And you have not told us! What do I call you now?'

The voice was faint, but Reverend Mother's face lighted up with pleasure.

'My dear Sir Andrew! Most hearty congratulations. How one rejoices to hear of the right thing being done. Prophecy may be the 'most gratuitous form of error', but I feel like Deborah.'

'You were always much too kind —'

'You were too modest — though it is a trait no one would wish to see altered. You will have heard, no doubt, that we are again in trouble?'

'But I hope not seriously?'

'A convent is like Cæsar's wife: it cannot afford to be breathed on. I am afraid we are in very serious trouble indeed. I do not yet know how serious it may prove to be. I confess I rang you up in order to consult you about it.'

'You could not please me more —'

It has been said that Reverend Mother was a consummate mistress of the spared word: she excelled herself as she now acquainted Sir Andrew Pearson with the facts. She could feel every point she made going right home to the astute and attentive ear which listened.

There was a moment's silence, and then Sir Andrew spoke.

'I think you have done very right to let me know, Reverend Mother. This is certainly a matter for us. I shall come down to Harrington —'

'Could you spare the time? This is more than I could have ventured to ask.' But the relief in Reverend Mother's voice was very great.

'Of course I shall come. My time exists for such troubles as this of yours. Besides —'

She knew he was searching around in his mind for a compliment sufficiently delicate, but much as she would have liked to hear it she could not wait.

'When will you come?'

'I will come at once. I will be with you in a few hours.'

8

Mr. Smith — of Birmingham

Meanwhile the Harrington police were very busy indeed.

The usual almost touching notices were got out inviting Juan Copanza to get in touch at once, and, with a view no doubt to the personal persuasion of any officer he might meet, a detailed description of him, obtained by Olive from Mother Assistant, was circulated to all stations.

The police have their own methods of letting it be known that they have a *corpus delicti* awaiting identification, and these were no sooner afoot than a certain Mrs. Parsley, together with her son Alfred, a lugubrious young man in the early twenties, and her pretty daughter Lulu, a 'teenager' (to use an expression which would have sent Mother Peagle stone deaf), arrived at the station, and were interviewed by Olive.

Mrs. Parsley began by stating that she was of the highest respectability and had never had dealings of any kind with the police before.

Mr. Alfred looked lugubrious, and Miss Lulu giggled, nudged her mother, and said, 'Come off it, Mum, now do.'

Nor, resumed Mrs. Parsley, would she be having dealings with the police now but that, in a moment of weakness and to oblige her son (here Mr. Alfred visibly wilted), she had so far forgotten her principles as to let a spare bedroom to a friend of his.

'Oh, come on, Mum, do.' And Miss Lulu, who was dying to tell the story herself, administered another nudge. But there was no hurrying Mrs. Parsley. Her point, however, when she came to it, was effective.

'I 'ave now reason to believe,' she said, 'that in admittin' this Mr. Smith into my 'ouse I admitted a corp.'

Miss Lulu laughed gaily, but Mr. Alfred was sunk in guilty gloom.

'Needless to say,' declared Mrs. Parsley, 'I didn't know the act I was committin', and would not have so done if 'e had given me the least reason to suspec'.'

Olive asked questions and showed photographs. A visit to the mortuary put the matter past all doubt.

The body on the dump and Mrs. Parsley's lodger, Mr. Smith — of Birmingham, she now supplemented — were one and the same.

'To think,' cried Mrs. Parsley, 'as 'e should 'ave deceived me in such a way —'

'Come off it, Mum. 'E wasn't a corp when 'e come into the 'ouse, or 'ow would 'e have been able to come? And now 'e is a corp 'e ain't in the 'ouse. So wot you got to grumble about?'

Olive could not feel that 'Mr. Smith — of Birmingham' carried her very far. Such a name and neighbourhood proclaimed itself as a hasty and impudent improvisation. Still, anything was better than nothing. The Parsleys could be closely examined about their late lodger, and his effects might yield much when inquired into.

Questioned by Olive: Mr. Alfred

admitted to knowing nothing about Mr. Smith. He had met him at the Party club meeting, where conversation had revealed them as kindred spirits. No, Smith wasn't young — not to say young: thirty-five if a day. He knew an awful lot, Smith did, and had travelled all over the earth. In fact, as Olive saw, Mr. Alfred had been fascinated.

Further questioned: Mr. Alfred knew of no enemies Mr. Smith could have had, and it was a shame if he had any.

Volunteered by Miss Lulu: Smith was a man likely to have as many enemies as there was people saw him.

Inserted by Mrs. Parsley: Miss Lulu was a naughty girl. Deceived as she might have been, Mrs. Parsley would always say of Mr. Smith that he was quite the gentleman. Or she would never have had him in her house, being accustomed to the highest standards. Mr. Alfred was to straighten his tie, and Miss Lulu to pull her frock down, for shame — what would the lady think?

Further questioned by Olive: Mr. Alfred couldn't rightly remember just how the matter arose of Smith's coming to board with them. Thought Smith had suggested it on hearing where Mr. Alfred lived.

Questioned by Olive: Yes, Mr. Alfred thought that was how it was. He would go so far as to say that was the way of it.

Questioned: Yes, now he came to think of it, Mr. Alfred was sure. Smith, on hearing Mr. Alfred lived in Harrington, had asked if he knew of any good rooms.

Volunteered by Miss Lulu: It was just like Mr. Alfred to be taken in. He always was. A complete softy, if you asked Miss Lulu. Luckily for all concerned, this streak showed only on the male side of the Parsley family.

Mr. Alfred: You shut up, Lu.

Miss Lulu: Shan't neither. Why did Flossy turn you down? Said you might be a moron.

Order being restored, Olive questioned Mrs. Parsley, who said she had always been of the highest respectability. No, Mr. Smith didn't go to business. Said he was a 'student'. Gave no trouble in the house but did not offer any help. Went out walks in the Lane. Silent usually, but chatty at table. No, never said much about hisself. She would go so far as to call him Sphinx-like. No, certainly wasn't English. Didn't give any special address in Birmingham. Never had any letters as she see, but might have gone to the Post for 'em. Never had any visitors at the 'ouse.

Miss Lulu by now positively raging to get her oar in, Olive transferred to her.

Examined by Olive: She would not be seventeen for some months, but sixteen was old enough to know a wrong 'un. Smith gave her the creeps. Not like a man except in some particulars, where only too much so. But not in a manly way. Ugh! Put her in mind of the 'pickshers'. Always a-creepin' and a-glidin' about. Never knew a man walk so soft. Thought he was an Indian.

It appeared that Miss Lulu had felt a loathing for the man from the start, and her evidence could be summed up in the vocable *Ugh!*

Olive's guardian angel in the shape of Sergeant Baseldon had been present at the interviews, acting as amanuensis; and when at last the Parsleys had gone their way, thanked, complimented, and enjoined to touch nothing of the dead man's effects until the police should have viewed them, he spoke.

'You done that real smart, little girl, as all you do is done smart. When that sort of people get jabberin' it's the deuce, like, but you got the one thing that needed gettin': that chap come to Harrington for a purpose. I'll bet you anything 'e picked up with young Parsley *after* he found out Parsley lived in Harrington. A nosin', creepin', glidin' sort of feller, so the girl says — and she's got the most sense of that little lot — 'e got shot when he was tryin' to bring off his purpose. Someone may 'ave been on the watch for 'im. Wot's your idea, pet?'

'I picked up the impression of a very unpleasant person. If so, I expect his purpose was unpleasant. If only we could get hold of Juan Copanza —'

'We will, love. Don't you fret. There's mills as grinds slow, like, but grinds exceedin' small.'

9

Better Late Than Never

People who are being talked about are said to suffer from burning ears: being prayed about must be different, for Verity was conscious of no such inconvenience while Mother Peagle 'earnestly reconsidered' her ribbonless estate.

It was Mother Peagle who did the suffering; for while it was true that the young Verity had been about as trying a little horror as ever afflicted a schoolmistress, still there was nothing in her record which is not common enough in children of exceptional vitality and impulses as yet unrestrained. Now, as Mother Peagle opened her heart to them, a hundred other memories of Verity came flooding back — of the child's pluck, of her affectionate and unresentful spirit, her eagerness at all times to give help, her quick intelligence and wit, her invariable generosity, her gift for leader-ship.

'God help us headmistresses,' Mother Peagle thought. 'We get very dull.'

And like a wise woman and a good nun she fell to her prayers.

It is the proud soul which goes on tormenting itself for error; the humble soul acknowledges human liability and seeks to make reparation. Mother Peagle rose from her knees to go straight to the cupboard where she kept, among much else, the sacred blue ribbons of office. They are handsome things, these blue ribbons: not frail trifles but a real investiture of dignity with their grand sweep from shoulder to hip. Seldom again in life shall virtue be so fitly adorned, authority find such circum-stance. Old women look back on these emblems. Princesses have been proud to wear them.

Mother Peagle took one out of the cupboard and laid it upon her table.

There was a tap on the door, and, upon permission, Philomene entered. Whatever she had come to say she did not say it; her whole attention was immediately focused on the ribbon.

Mother Peagle never dissembled. She did not even ask what Philomene had come about, for it was plain Philomene had totally forgotten. All she said was:

'Do you know where Verity is, dear?'

Philomene's words came tumbling out.

'I *think* she's in her room. I *think* she's going out for a walk. But I *think* I could catch her —'

'Run, dear, and see if you can. Ask her to come to me for a minute —'

Philomene was gone.

Girls of Verity's age were allowed to go out by themselves once or twice a week, and Verity was discovered in neat walking trim when Philomene burst in upon her. She would have been gone already but that she was not quite sure of the hang of her skirt.

'Hallo, Phil. *Some* people knock at doors before entering. As you *are* here you might have a look at this beastly skirt —'

'It only wants —' And Philomene

adroitly did it, remarking with studied nonchalance:

'The Peaglums wants to see you for a minute —'

'Bother the Peaglums! Does she expect me to keep my boy-friend waiting? What does she want?'

'How should I know? Where *are* you going?'

'Now then, nosey. But if you must know, I am going to see that rich old cousin of mine — the one from whom I have 'expectations'.'

Philomene sighed. She knew this cousin of old. There 'wasn't no sich a person', but whenever she was invoked it meant that Verity did not want any company. Philomene had wept quarts over that cousin in her day.

'Don't forget the Peaglums. Oh — and, Verity —'

'What's the matter now?'

'Why are you so horrid to me?'

'Don't be maudlin. I'm not.'

'Yes, you are. We've never been out together once this term. We used to be such friends.'

'Circumstances alter cases. It's you that's horrid to me really — always about with Torquilla and Alauda. Besides, you're a Ribbon. You might go giving me away.'

'Verity. I'd never. Not if I was stuck all over blue ribbons back and front. I only go with Torquilla because — because you've chucked me —'

'There, there. Of course you wouldn't, Phil; I know that. Still, things can't be quite the same when one of us is a Ribbon and the other isn't —'

'Suppose you were a Ribbon too?'

'Suppose I were the Queen —'

'No, but seriously, Verity?'

'My child, when the Peaglums makes me a Ribbon it will be a sign we mustn't expect to have her with us much longer. Don't be morbid.'

'Oh, Verity, you are funny. I like you ever so much better than anyone else —'

'Better than Prudence? You shock me. Oh well. I suppose I'd better go and feel the Peaglums' pulse. You've made me nervous about her.'

'Yes, do. I'll wait for you here. Perhaps

you'll let me come on your walk with you then.'

'No pathos, please. Ribbons should be made of sterner stuff.'

'Oh, shut up about Ribbons. Go and see the Peaglums.'

Verity went; not sorry, on the whole, to show off the new suit. She had not the faintest presentiment of what was afoot, and so was 'struck all of a heap' when the Peaglums came straight to the point.

'Verity dear, you are the new Ribbon. Here it is, and may God bless you.'

Verity recoiled. 'Mother —'

Mother Peagle went calmly on. 'Torquilla and all the other Ribbons asked me to do this. On thinking it over I have felt sure they were right. It sometimes happens to strong characters, dear, to get misjudged. I have allowed myself to act with prejudice against you, and I am sorry.'

'Don't, Mother — please —'

Mother Peagle patted Verity's hand and took up the ribbon.

'Here it is. I realize it comes too late to give the pleasure it might have done —'

'No. I like it this way.'

'I would put it on for you,' Mother Peagle said, 'if you were not so very smart. What a nice suit, Verity.'

'Do you think so? The skirt is a bit — it's apt to show my slip —'

'It won't when you are wearing the right sort of underclothes to go with it.' And Mother Peagle gave the waist a much more competent adjustment than Philomene had been able to.

'You're a wonder, Mother. Being a nun too — I beg your pardon —'

'My dear, I knew all about frocks and suits before you were born or thought of. Off with you now, and have your walk. Remember, that ribbon takes effect as from the time when you should have had it. It makes you next to Torquilla and Alauda.'

She shook both Verity's hands and kissed her.

Smart as the new suit was, and slightly absurd as the new ribbon looked over it, none the less it was in this motley that Verity burst in again upon the waiting Philomene.

'My worst fears are confirmed. Pray for the poor dear Peaglums, Phil; she is slipping fast away.'

'Oh — Verity —'

'Don't be lachrymose. Come on, let's go for that walk — though I did promise my cousin —'

★ ★ ★

It was when they were coming back after the walk. A 'definitely super' car was standing outside the Convent door. Not that this was anything out of the way, but there was something *different* about this car.

'I hope Inez isn't worse and it's a specialist,' Philomene said.

Verity was positive. 'Awful big shot, but not a doctor.'

The 'awful big shot' was about to descend from his chariot, the door of which was held open for him by two rigid figures at the salute.

'Coo!' murmured Philomene.

The big shot drew himself up to a tall but tenuous height on the pavement. The early twilight of an autumn day was falling, but the ray of a street lamp shone on the face.

Verity clutched Philomene by the elbow.

'See who it is, Phil?'

'No. And yet I —'

The door was opened, showing a vision of Mother Peck. The big shot stepped inside. The door was closed.

'The plot thickens!' Verity whispered in a thrilling tone. ' 'Ancestral voices prophesying war.' *It's Mr. Pearson!*'

10

The Visit to the Parsley House

Olive and Sergeant Baseldon were on their way to inspect the Parsley 'home' and the late Mr. Smith's effects.

As they went Olive continued to fret about the disappearance of Juan Copanza, who continued to resist all calls to come and make friends with the police.

'A man can't just vanish into thin air. I have a feeling that Copanza never existed. The nuns imagined him.'

As there was no one about the Sergeant permitted himself to be unofficial; he took and patted Olive's hand.

'Trouble with you girls,' he said, 'isn't that you ain't clever, it's you're too eager. You feel things as too personal. What you've got to do, if you're ever to be the first lady Chief Inspector, as the Missus and me both thinks you will be, is to keep calm. That's the great lesson every policeman 'as to learn.'

'I don't think I shall ever be a Chief Inspector,' Olive said.

'You mean as you'll get married?'

'No —'

'What, then?'

'I — I don't know —'

The Parsley residence bore witness to the respectability of the family by being detached. In design it was of almost unprecedented hideousness even as villa residences go, but it stood alone, surrounded by a garden which was full of nothing but crazy pavement. Mr. Alfred had designed it.

Olive at once noted, and pointed out to the Sergeant, that the house was, as the crow flies, no distance at all away from the Convent and the walls which surrounded its demesne.

The police visitors were happy enough to find only Miss Lulu at home, and she seemed delighted to see them. There were 'no flies' on this young lady.

'Called 'isself a 'stoodent'. 'E was no more a 'stoodent' nor what I am. If you ast me, I'd say 'e was a spy — Bolshy spy.'

It should be said that Miss Lulu, at sixteen, supplemented her extensive lack of experience by what she saw at the 'pickshers'. But her spy theory was not altogether based on photographic melodrama; she drew attention to Mr. Smith's small outfit of clothes, from every garment of which the maker's name, together with all other marks of identification, had been removed.

'Quite the gentleman!' she mimicked her mother, with that sad lack of filial respect so characteristic of her generation, which certainly cannot expect to 'live long in the land'.

'It's in 'ere you want to 'ave a look.' And Miss Lulu, pulling aside a curtain, revealed what was without doubt an interesting piece of luggage. It was a small case made of some metal and most meticulously locked, padlocked and tied with strong cord.

'I'd take care if I was you,' counselled Lulu. 'A Bolshy spy, that's wot 'e was.' And she ducked down behind the bed while the Sergeant coped with the exhibit.

But nothing startling occurred when

the case at last stood open. Inside was much paper scrawled over in a language totally unfamiliar to Olive. It was not even in Roman characters. More interesting was a map, which appeared to be of the Convent walls, with special attention to those parts where a builder's care was needed. There was also a passport, emanating from St. Helena, made out in the name of 'John Smith, Student, British Subject', and showing a not very recognizable photograph of the same.

It was, however, under all the literary matter, and flat with the bottom of the case, that the real interest was found. Here was another case, not much larger than a pencil-box, and again closely secured. This, when the Sergeant had opened it with the utmost caution, was found to contain a very queer collection of objects. These were a sort of sturdy blowpipe and a number of highly pointed darts.

'Don't you go touchin' 'em,' cried Miss Lulu. 'The points is all over a vegytable fat of the most deadly poisonous properties, which bein' interduced into

the blood-stream by the smallest perfora-
tion causes instant-an-ous coma and
death.'

She had got all this from a thrilling and
highly illustrated brochure given away in
connection with a recent picture dealing
with Mexico. But the darts, when
examined later at Scotland Yard, were
found to correspond exactly with the
information.

Something about the sheer devilishness
of all this had a profoundly chastening
effect on Olive and the Sergeant. It was as
though the authentic jungle surrounded
them, there amid the hire-purchasings of
that mean little bedroom. Was there, or
was there not, a faint but evil smell from
those darts? The Sergeant made haste to
repack the case with a view to removal,
while Olive put a few more questions to
the spritely Lulu.

'Did — Mr. Smith — go out and about
much?'

'Out, but not about. I kep' me eye on
'im. Mousin' up and down the Lane —'

Olive made a wild shot. 'Did you, by
any chance, ever see the young man that

was gardener at the Convent?'

'I thought it was ol' man Turtle —'

'This was his assistant. A young man — a Spaniard, I believe. Juan Copanza?'

Miss Lulu wrinkled her brows.

'Come to think of it, I believe I did see a young fella once. Come over the garden wall quick, 'e did, almost as if 'e jumped it. Some champion 'urdler —'

'When was this? How long ago?'

'About a week —'

'Was — Smith — in the Lane at the time?'

'Yes, 'e was. Mousin' as usual. I 'ad an idea the young fella wanted a look at 'im —'

'Do you think he got one?'

'I'd say 'e did.'

'What you are telling me may be of the greatest importance —'

'Oo, er —'

'Can you remember anything else?'

Lulu giggled.

'Yes — 'cos I 'ad to laugh. Smith see the young fella come over the wall, and — 'ave you ever see a big spider leg it? Well, that's wot Smith done — sort of stoopin' and lurkin' and 'uggin' the wall. An' nex' minute 'e was back 'ere, a-tryin' to give me a kiss — ugh! But I fetched 'im a good 'un with the rollin'-pin. Coo! but I did 'ave to laugh —'

11

'O Cuckoo! Shall I Call Thee Bird,
or but a Wandering Voice?'

Olive and the Sergeant took a short-cut back to the station through the Convent grounds.

The season was autumn, and not now of 'mellow fruitfulness' but inclining towards winter. The sky above was leaden; and though everything seemed perfectly still, none the less an occasional *frisson* of cold air was about, nipping some sere leaf here and there to the ground.

'I hate autumn,' Olive said.

'Come now, you've no call to do that, girl. If there was no autumn there'd be no spring.'

The Sergeant was carrying Mr. Smith's metal case, and he referred to that when he said:

'Queer sort of thing. I don't remember

ever to have seen its like. I think the fellow must have been a Mexican. It's in Mexico where they use blowguns.'

'And in other parts of South America,' Olive said.

The Sergeant shook his head. 'Ah, I know very little about them other parts. America means Yanks to me. There's Argentine though, isn't there? And a place called Chilly — though I'm told it's 'ot as blazes —'

'Yes. And Brazil,' Olive said. 'And there's Anaconda —'

'Never heard any good of any of it,' said the Sergeant.

They were passing round the little lake in the grounds as they spoke, and Olive paused to watch the zigzag patterns of one or two moorhens on the water.

The Sergeant glanced at her suspiciously. 'You're tired. Let's sit down on one o' these benches for a minute.'

They sat in companionable silence. But then Olive quoted in an undertone:

'The sedge is withered from the lake,
And no birds sing.'

'You couldn't 'ardly expect 'em to sing all year round,' said the Sergeant. 'They'd bust 'emselves.'

He had hardly spoken when the loud, clear call of a bird rang out over the grounds.

Olive sprang to her feet. Less nimbly the Sergeant rose and stood beside her.

The call was repeated.

'Whatever —?' Olive cried. 'It's like the cuckoo and the curlew, but with more notes. Couldn't you swear it was telling something?'

'That's no English bird,' said the Sergeant. 'Got loose out of an aviary, that has.' His police conscience rousing within him, he added:

'We ought to get a-hold of it if we can. Maybe it comes from the Zoo —'

'But — where is it?'

They scanned the skies, the trees, the bushes, but not a trace of the bird was to be seen.

Children, and one or two nuns, emerged from the house and stood, also listening. Windows were thrown up, and heads appeared at them.

Again the bird called. And then burst into a passionate warble like the nightingale. Olive was right: one could have sworn it was telling something —

Time passed, and the bird ceased. The children ran hither and thither searching for a sight of it and trying to imitate its call.

But it was not heard again.

As Olive and the Sergeant resumed their way, Mother Assistant was seen to come out, and to her Olive at once ran.

'Did you hear it, Mother?'

'I did indeed. I never heard anything like it. The children are trying to look it up in the library, but without any luck —'

'Did you feel, as I did, that it was — sort of — talking to someone?'

Mother Assistant nodded emphatically.

'That is exactly the impression I got. Who knows? 'There are more things in heaven and earth —' Mother Infirmarian tells me it had the best effect on our poor little Inez —'

12

Sir Andrew Pearson

Sir Andrew Pearson was not a Prodigal Son — far from it — but if he had been, and were returning now, husk-sated, to the paternal mansion, he could not have been more kindly received than he was by Mother Peck.

One gathers from the parable that the elder gentleman, the father of the Prodigal Son, was well able to express emotion. This gift was denied Mother Peck. Some even thought her deficient. But she opened the Convent door on Sir Andrew that night in a way which nailed that calumny to the counter for ever as the false-hood which it was.

'I am pleased to see you, Sir Andrew. I trust you are in good health?'

The lay-sister in attendance gasped for breath: Mother Peck had not withheld the favour of her hand.

Nor did Sir Andrew show himself unequal to this high moment; he grasped the hand and swept a bow over it.

'I am very well indeed, thank you, Mother. But how are *you?*'

'I am well, in the mercy of God.'

There was a short religious pause.

'It looks,' said Mother Peck, as she closed the door, 'as if we were to have a fog, Sir Andrew.'

'I fear so indeed, Mother. Turning colder too.'

'These are small trials, Sir Andrew. If we were to be tried according to our desserts, which of us could abide it?'

'Which indeed, Mother?' Sir Andrew stood first on one leg and then on the other.

'Be pleased,' said Mother Peck, 'to step this way.' And all the angels of God sang together as she added:

'Reverend Mother is expecting you.'

There was no anticlimax. No further words were spoken as the solemn progress towards Reverend Mother's parlour was begun. But Mother Peck was edified to behold how Sir Andrew remembered the way without fault, traversed it with ceremony, and drew up as upon a chalked line.

Sir Andrew would have been glad, no doubt, had he known, the edification he was causing; but the truth is that memory was making such an attack on his feelings he was hardly conscious of Mother Peck, five foot full as she was. He had once been so very happy here. The words of de Musset haunted his mind:

'A Saint Blaise, à la Zuecca,
Le cœur est bien là.'

Nothing was altered in this timeless place. There was a lump in his throat as he inhaled again the hallows of the chapel, as he saw again the bright beam which denoted the Grotto of Lourdes, as he heard the muted recital of that organ which it seemed Mother Frederica had never given up playing.

There came to him too, out of the warm darkness which stretched beyond the cloister, a sense of the volume of young life invisibly present there.

He did not need Mother Peck to chasten him.

Mother Peck now began her great act. She withdrew from the door, she stealthily approached the door, she listened at the door — she tapped at the door. She listened again.

'*Entrez* — '

The door might now be canonically opened, and with a fine flourish it was.

'Reverend Mother — Sir Andrew Pearson —'

Then, with one of her throttled curtsies and a look of adoration in her sea-green eye, Mother Peck withdrew.

'Some day you will come here and find me not able to be got at at all,' Reverend Mother said, as she and Sir Andrew shook hands with an exchange of cordial glances. 'I am more and more hemmed in by ritual. My impulse was to meet you in the porch this evening, but I should have sent Mother Peck to bed for a fortnight if I had done. I expect you get the same sort of thing at the Yard nowadays?'

'I think not the same sort of thing. If you will excuse me, how — er — well you are looking and — ah — how *young* —'

She laughed. 'I will let you into the secret of our youth. It is the bonnet —'

'The bonnet —'

'The bonnet. It is far better than expensive beauty treatments; it conceals our grey hair and supports our tissues.'

The entrance of Sister Carmela with the tea-tray interrupted his protests. At sight of her old friend again, and on hearing of his change of style, five minutes hardly sufficed for the Sister's glowing Maltese raptures.

It was when tea was over, and the Sister gone, that Sir Andrew, speaking in a low voice, came to the point.

'Let us go over the facts again. Tell me, how is Inez?'

'She is — very ill.'

'Physically?'

'The primary is mental. Terror —'

'That is dreadful. When did this state of terror begin?'

'On the day of the discovery of the body on the dump. That was the day also of the disappearance of Juan Copanza.'

Sir Andrew sat in rapid thought.

'I believe,' he said, 'the discovery was for a time kept a secret from the children. How did this child come to know of it?'

'That, I am afraid, I do not know. She was, I may say, a great friend of Copanza's.'

'When was Copanza last certainly seen?'

'I do not know of anyone who saw him later than Inez herself. She asked permission to go down the garden to see him shortly before supper. She was gone a good long while. On her return it was noticed that she looked pale and dazed, and could eat no supper.'

'Reverend Mother, who was this Copanza? Did you absolutely trust him?'

'My dear Sir Andrew, would I have employed him here unless? I had the best references with him and found him more than satisfactory. He was a stand-by. I may say I had myself a strong personal liking for him. I shall find it very hard to believe anything against him.'

'That is much in his favour. And yet,' Sir Andrew said, 'there is a dead body, and he takes at once to flight. Before that some words spoken by him to a child, and the child is terrified. After his disappearance she is more terrified still. Upon my word, I do not like the works of Copanza. As for Inez, she must be reassured. She must be told that she is in a country where an immense force exists for the express purpose that she shall not be terrified. I — and all that I represent — have no greater duty than to cherish and protect her. Upon my word —'

But Reverend Mother's voice was eerie in answer. 'She no longer believes what one tells her. Her mind has reverted — to Anaconda — to panic — the panic of the jungle. I, God help me, have never seen — primitive terror — before. It is enough to deceive even the — elect. What can be done?'

'Much can be done. You and I together, we shall do it. Leave the practical side entirely to me. I beg you to put your mind at rest. I shall put through a call to the Yard — now. Then — may I speak to Inez?'

'Certainly. I will fetch her. You must prepare to be shocked —'

He put through his call shortly. When he had done so he stood looking all round the beautiful room where he was. The picture it presented was one of perfect security in a well-ordered and enduring scheme of things.

But the eeriness dwelt.

13

Inez

'Come, dear —'

Reverend Mother was back in the great parlour, bringing with her a shrunk and shrinking figure which at first Sir Andrew could hardly have recognized.

Indeed, it was some time before he could see Inez, who crouched on the floor in the shadows and could not be persuaded to come forward.

Poor child, she had reasons enough for not wishing to appear: her face was swollen with crying, her mouth warped, her lovely eyes were almost brute in their pain, her skin was blotched, her hair a tangle and a mat. Yet at sight of Sir Andrew she did make some forlorn effort to pull herself together and stand up straight.

Sir Andrew was quick to notice these favourable signs and to take advantage of them. He drew himself up to his full height beside the girl, gently patted her shoulder and took her hand. He himself wiped her face with an enormous, spotlessly clean handkerchief he produced.

'Oh,' she moaned, 'I am ashamed —' But she clung to the handkerchief.

'Nonsense,' he said. 'It's only me. You remember me?'

'I — I do not forget, señor —'

'I should hope not. I am here to take every scrap of fear and trouble away from you. All you have to do is to help me by giving me your confidence. You will soon be feeling better. There is always help. Remember that: there is always help.'

Reverend Mother, who had been quietly smoothing the girl's hair, now ceased, and rose.

'Yes, dear, there is always help. And now I want you to have a talk with Sir Andrew alone. He is your best friend just now. Try to tell him as much as you can. I shall be close at hand. God bless you.'

She kissed Inez and quietly left the room.

'We are alone now —' Sir Andrew was beginning.

'Ah,' she cried, 'how do you know?'

He was for a moment abashed, so eerie was her voice. He took her hands again, shocked at the coldness of them.

'Do you think we are not?'

'Oh God, if I could know —'

'Would you like more light?'

But she shrank back into the dark corner. 'No — no more light —'

'Now, dear,' he said, standing closely beside her, 'there is no hurry. Try to relax yourself. Listen quietly to me. You are among the best and kindest of friends, each one of whom would gladly give her life to save yours; and all around you, endlessly watchful though you cannot see it, is the whole power of the law of a great country. Put it out of your head that you are in any danger.'

'Danger —' she muttered. And, her eyes awfully dilating, she looked him in the face.

He observed her closely. There was lucidity again in her eye, almost a cunning; but he could not disguise from himself, and was puzzled and even hurt, that she profoundly mistrusted him.

'You are great man of de police,' she said. 'But in England all things are different from Anaconda —'

'I know,' he said. 'That is why I so much need your help to help you —'

'Was he not covered with de brown paper?' she cried. 'What more could Diego do? Is it wrong, in England, to kill a snake which is about to bite?'

Sir Andrew carefully abstained from asking who 'Diego' was, or what the 'brown paper'.

'Did Diego kill a snake?' was all he said. 'Did you see him do it?'

She nodded. 'It was a man-snake. Dey are the worst. It was killing me, but Diego shot it. Is it wrong to kill a man-snake?'

'Not if you know it is one, and there is nothing else you can do —'

'You do not put people in prison for killing man-snakes?'

'No, no, dear. Diego has nothing to fear. We shall only ask him to explain.'

Sir Andrew was back on his old and successful policy, of trusting the innate tendency of all human stories to tell themselves if they are treated with that meekness which 'inherits the earth'. Inez's face lost its cunning look, she drew closer to him. Undoubtedly she was about to give him her confidence —

But then suddenly her manner changed. She lifted a finger — '*Hush* —' He saw the terror return to her face.

He was now able to watch one of these fits in action. He saw how she sought frantically around for cover but found none adequate to her needs, at which her agony increased. He saw it was not imagination which caused her panic, and it was not hysterical: it was more like a telepathy — a remotely atavistic warning, coeval with the cavemen, crucifying the nerves with foreknowledge of danger and doom.

'Ah,' she cried, 'de window — de window —' And she threw herself in a crouched heap down in a corner.

'It is nothing,' he reassured her. 'A pane of the fanlights must have got loose. It is far too high for anyone to get up there from outside.'

'Down!' she whispered. 'Down upon de floor. An Anacondan can climb anywhere —'

There was now no doubt of a stealthy sound at the top of the great window. Even as Sir Andrew stood gazing the curtain shivered and seemed to travel slightly on its brass rings.

'Hallo, you up there. What are you doing?' And, grasping his ebony cane, Sir Andrew sprang at the window.

Instantly the curtain was swept aside. One of the smaller casements at the top was thrown open and a great piece of brown paper flopped oddly on the floor inside.

A voice spoke.

'We give you back the brown paper, Diego —'

Then — *zip, zip* — two bullets passed over the prostrate body of Inez in the corner, and — *zip* — a third buried itself in the wainscot hardly an inch beyond her head.

There might have been a fourth and fatal shot but that Sir Andrew, seizing the weapon nearest to his hand, some uncouth trophy of African missions, sent it hurtling in the direction of the sniper. His aim was true; the heavy object carried away casement and all, and came crashing to earth outside. He opened the window and rushed out. But thick darkness met him — darkness and fog. Nothing was to be seen, and not a sound to be heard.

Re-entering the room, he found that Reverend Mother had returned and was kneeling in the corner beside Inez, feeling her pulse.

The girl lay in marvellous beauty — too lovely. Sir Andrew had little hope.

'Is — is she —?'

'No. She has fainted.'

There was a loud rustling on the floor. It was the brown paper, which seemed to heave and move towards them — to have become alive —

Reverend Mother exclaimed with horror.

Sir Andrew Pearson did not hesitate. He snatched up Inez from the floor, gave her into Reverend Mother's arms, and pushed — actually pushed — Reverend Mother to the door. Then he turned, and with his ebony cane beat down the deadly South American snake which reared itself, furiously hissing, from the many folds of the fibrous paper.

'I do beg your pardon, Reverend Mother,' he said, 'for pushing you.'

14

An Ethical Point Resolved by Fog

Psychology, more or less erroneous, is often invoked to eke out the interest of a story, but ethics hardly ever. Nevertheless, after the events of that evening, a serious ethical consideration confronted Reverend Mother.

The School for which she was responsible consisted of not less than, say, one hundred and forty girls aged from seventeen to seven. If a very fierce measles had broken out in the School, or a scarlet fever, those children not involved would have been sent home. No measles or scarlet fever formed the present crisis, but a campaign of murder directed against one child might very well involve some one or other of the remaining hundred and thirty-nine.

Suppose, for example, that snake, so effectively dealt with by Sir Andrew

Pearson, had got loose in the Junior School? And who could positively say what more was coming?

Reverend Mother must ask herself, therefore, if it was fair play to the parents and common honesty to keep the children at school?

She knew perfectly well that if, say, the Lady Gale got so much as an inkling in Bordighera of what was happening in Harrington, then the very latest development in jet-propulsion — said to be saucer-shaped and capable of doing its 1,500 m.p.h. — would not be nearly fast enough to bring her to Alauda's side.

Gaelic is no doubt a rich and expressive tongue — as much richer than the Sassenach as the works of Ossian are obviously superior to those of Shakespeare — but Gaelic itself would fail to express the feelings of the MacBinkie of MacBinkie if he knew that his Thistle had been even for a moment on the same premises as a poisonous snake.

Admiral Hercules would certainly have a fit.

Reverend Mother could not doubt that, at the least hint, all the parents would arise as one parent and descend in a parental avalanche upon Harrington, all saying the same thing, and saying it very loud and clear, and shouting it in Reverend Mother's ear.

Most of the parents were earnest students of crime in its fictional form; but in factual form, and as concerning the flesh of their flesh, their horror of it would outdo that of every Chief Justice who has ever dismissed a murder appeal with an apophthegm.

But first things come first; and the first thing was to get Inez back (as they put it in Guernsey) 'in bed with the doctor', a nun forever by her side, and two stout detectives from Scotland Yard cutting off all access by their bulk alone.

Not a child in the School had a suspicion of what had occurred or how near they were to a sudden outburst of the Christmas holidays.

Of the Community, Mother Assistant knew, Mother Peagle, and, probably, Mother Bunting as novice-mistress. But such shining lights as Mother Peck and Mr. Turtle were left in total darkness: all of which goes to show how very much may be happening under the noses of intelligent people and they knowing nothing about it.

The telephone-call put through to the Yard immediately before the outrage now began to have effect in the arrival at Harrington of a choice selection from among the brainiest and weightiest of the Chief Detective-Inspectors and Super-Superintendents of the former place. Assembled together in the Priests' Parlour, they looked like a grounded school of porpoises, each grasping under an immense fin the squashiest of squash hats.

'Well, gentlemen —' And Sir Andrew made his appearance among them, to a buzz of acclaim.

'I hope,' he went on, 'none of you had any difficulty in getting here? The fog is very dense, I'm afraid.'

'Aye,' said a very Scots voice. 'It's that, Sir Andrew. I would feel justified in calling it dense, and I misdoot it'll maybe be worse. I'm fearing we're in for a long spell of it.'

And Superintendent MacTavish loudly and gloomily blew his nose.

'I sincerely hope you are mistaken, MacTavish,' said Sir Andrew, 'for I have a matter to put before you all this evening which fog would greatly complicate. However, it cuts both ways, I suppose: what hinders us, hinders — other people.'

'I'm seeing your point, Sir Andrew; but I'm nae so sure I'm agreeing — speaking with respect. Bad is bad at the best of times, and a wheen extra bad, such as a fog noo, is always a point against law and order.'

'There's logic in what ye say, MacTavish,' put in another voice, highly reminiscent of Aberdeen.

'Well, we must hope for the best. Meanwhile, Reverend Mother wishes us to begin our conference with dinner — and perhaps a 'wee drappie' which may remind some of you of before the Kaiser's war —'

There was a chorus of approval.

Meanwhile, in what Shakespeare might have called 'another part of the wood', the whole of Harrington being now more or less of a dark and dubious wood, Reverend Mother also was holding a council. It had to be short, inasmuch as it consisted of all the nuns in key positions, of whom none liked to stay long from her post.

Hence Reverend Mother spoke urgently, the point she raised being the break-up of the School until better times.

'We cannot doubt what the parents would wish. We dare no longer take the risk of not informing them. True, we cannot give them the facts, and we shall have to face a good deal of complaint and adverse criticism. I will word a circular letter —'

'What will you say, Reverend Mother, if I may ask? It is such an unprecedented thing, apart from epidemic —'

'I shall say that, until a matter connected with a foreign child is settled, both the Foreign Office and Scotland Yard advise a short suspension of the School.'

'It is for you to say, Reverend Mother. Perhaps, if we postponed the matter for a day or two, the necessity need not arise.'

'We *must* postpone it,' Reverend Mother said, 'until this fog lifts. It would be a practical impossibility to get the children off. But I shall have my letter in readiness, and, if tomorrow gives us any hope, it must be sent, and preparations made accordingly.'

'Of course,' boomed Mother Assistant in her best brigadier voice — the same which had hopelessly bamboozled Sergeant Baseldon.

Reverend Mother then withdrew to draft her letter, which cost her immense pains. And she knew there could be no sleep in prospect for her that night, but she must pass its anxious hours ceaselessly patrolling the dormitories, pulling aside curtains to peer into cubicles, and ever and anon reverting to the infirmary for the latest report on Inez.

That letter was one of the hardest tasks which Reverend Mother of Harrington had ever had to undertake.

And it was destined never to be sent.

15

The Presence of Sister Ursula

The night passed without further event. Yet there was nothing to show in the morning that it had passed. The fog was as dense as ever.

Mercifully it did not afflict the spirits of the children at Harrington, who found it exciting to have all the lights on at breakfast-time. Mass was felt to be a midnight Mass. No human power could have prevented Fr. Witherstick's punctual arrival to say that Mass, and, the Mass said, nothing could have prevented his departure. But first a little procession of senior nuns accompanied him to the infirmary, where Inez was communicated. Her condition on this morning of all mornings seemed to be quieter.

All London was coping as best as it could with this periodic nuisance which it brings down on itself. Nothing quite like a fog in an English city has ever been known, probably, in history. Mists are inevitable in a damp island, and were known in the days of Beowulf. But a fog is a result of highly artificial conditions — of industrialism, of factories and great smoke-stacks and of myriads of domestic chimneys, all hard at it, day and night befouling the air, until the higher atmosphere becomes choked with it; then, owing to some change of temperature, it is held and forced down again to meet and mix with the ascending mists of the foul dank fens and rivers, and the light of the sun is utterly blocked out.

A London fog is simply the dense saturated mists of the sea blackened by the pent-up smoke of our innumerable chimneys.

In such a fog the pedestrian may be turned right round and set off in the reverse direction without in the least knowing what he is doing.

Business, of course, every kind of human activity, is enormously complicated by fog. Nevertheless it has to be gone about somehow: during the night the 'big shots' of Scotland Yard managed to disperse, so that in the morning only Sir Andrew and Superintendent MacTavish remained to partake of the breakfast which Sister Carmela brought them.

Mr. MacTavish was to be in command of all police arrangements at Harrington throughout the day. He therefore made an excellent breakfast.

'I'm fearing,' he remarked to Sir Andrew, 'that there'll be no evacuating the bits of lasses from this Schule today. So if you'll be introducing me to the Reverend Mother body, Sir Andrew —'

The 'Reverend Mother body' was soon on the spot, where Mr. MacTavish addressed her as 'Your Reverend Leddyship', and showed a degree of cheerful resourcefulness and perfect confidence which was entirely after her mind.

'If we canna remove the Schule as far as maybe we would like, your Leddyship,' said Mr. MacTavish, 'we'll be removing it at least as far as we can. Sir Andrew here has been telling me of a grand New Building you have and a fine Coronation Wing. It was my idea, if Your Reverend

Leddyship was to agree, that the weans might be using them for their lessons and games the day. That way they'll no be seeing the police bodies as will maybe be aroond doon here, and where the eye doesna see the heart doesna fash itself.'

Reverend Mother began to feel that a day passed with Superintendent MacTavish might have compensations.

'And don't you think,' Sir Andrew said, addressing her, 'that Inez herself might be better altogether away from this part of the house?'

Reverend Mother's mind passed immediately to some rooms in the New Building which had sometimes been used for isolation purposes. They were cut off by a separate staircase and a corridor. Their windows were high and not easily visible. 'Anacondans can climb anywhere — ' So Inez had been proud of saying. But even Anacondans could hardly climb in at a window they could not see. In one of these rooms, with a nun constantly in and out, and with her armed detectives just outside the door, Inez would be far safer than in the infirmary.

They were all three discussing the advisability of such a change when it occurred to them all that a Sister was in the room, Sister Ursula, moving soundlessly as she cleared the breakfast things from the table.

It would never have occurred to Sir Andrew that a Sister might be a source of danger, and Reverend Mother had not noticed; but MacTavish jerked an elbow in her direction with a murmured, 'Whisht —'

'Your Reverend Leddyship will excuse me,' he said to Reverend Mother when Sister Ursula had withdrawn, 'but holy as yon body looks, and nae doot is, ye cannot be too canny whom ye let into your confidence. Masel' noo, if an angel from heaven was to come into ma wee cuddie-hole at the Yard while I was discussing a case, I would ask yon angel to step ootby until I was done.'

'It was inexcusably careless of me,' Reverend Mother said.

'Na, na. Your Leddyship hasna had the reasons for suspeeciousness which an auld detective body comes tae have.'

'I am not so sure, Mr. MacTavish. I have had to do with girls for many years —'

'Och, the wee lasses —' was the indulgent response.

'Besides, you don't understand, Mac-Tavish,' said Sir Andrew, a little impatiently. He was annoyed at such a gross error in himself, and at exposing himself, Deputy Commissioner as he was, to the rebuke of a Superintendent.

'Most of these lay-sisters,' he went on, 'hardly speak English. And they never heed a word that is said — too busy saying their Rosaries. That's what they do while about their work, isn't it, Reverend Mother?'

'Theoretically, Sir Andrew. Sir Andrew is always too kind to us religious,' she explained to Mr. MacTavish.

'Hoots, toots, Your Leddyship, I hae nae doots he's aboot right. I'm a Presbyteerian masel', but I can appreciate the beauties of the auld kirk of Rome. And to think she would be saying her Rosary noo, and me not knowing.'

'You must let us show you how it is

done, Mr. MacTavish. It is really very practical, and I think might appeal to a Presbyterian. But, whether Sister Ursula was saying her Rosary or not, I feel quite sure we need fear nothing from her.'

'I am sure we need not,' said Sir Andrew, and he rose to his feet.

'Well, I suppose I must be making a dash for it now. I am leaving you in the best of hands, Reverend Mother. Mac here is not the man to be frightened of a few Anacondans, eh, Mac?'

'I couldna rightly say, Sir Andrew, never to my knowledge having set eyes on yin. But I'm no easy to be frichted — unless it might be yin o' these unco' spiders with the gey lang legs —'

Reverend Mother had turned to Sir Andrew. 'When I think of last night —'

He blushed with delight. 'You are always far too kind. I did — er — nothing — ah — nothing. To serve you in any way —' He broke off, and added:

'I shall get back here, somehow, to-night —'

He turned on MacTavish.

'And let me find, Mac, that you are

well ahead with the Rosary.'

'Dinna fash yersel', mon,' was the reply.

And it was adopted as the motto for the day.

16

The Coronation Wing

Philomene was up early that morning and, quickly getting dressed, went into Verity's room, which was next to hers.

She found that young lady fast asleep. Philomene shook her.

'Verity. Verity, wake up. Do you mean to tell me you don't know what day it is?'

'Haven't the foggiest —?'

She might well say the 'foggiest'!

She sat up at once. 'What a super fog! I do like a real good fog.'

'So do I. There's nothing I like better. Get up now. I'm going to dress you and finish up with *it*!'

'What's 'it'?'

'Your ribbon, you cuckoo!'

Verity remembered, and stood stock still until the great moment came and she was told to 'Duck your head, you donkey, I can't get up so high'.

'Oh, it does look super. I wish mine was as new.' And Philomene smoothed it down back and front and arranged the fringe on the thigh.

'What a bore there's such a fog I can't see it properly. If there's one thing I bar it's a fog,' Verity declared.

'Yes. And these convent glasses! Let's go along to the hair-washing place and have a decent look.'

'Yes, let's.'

It was pitch-dark in the corridors, and the first thing they did in their haste was to collide with something so solid that they knew it at first bump for Torquilla.

'Torquilla. Really, you want a whole school to yourself —'

Torquilla showed not the slightest sympathy. She never did.

'*Vanitas vanitatum!*' she remarked. 'Well, you can't just now. The Peaglums had a brain-storm in the night, and the only thing which would calm her down this morning was to call a Ribbons' Meeting.'

'A Ribbons' Meeting!'

'A meeting,' Torquilla explained, 'of

Ribbons. Otherwise she gets melancholia with hootings. The doctor says she may become dangerous if not indulged.'

Such a thing was without precedent.

What was more, this meeting was not to be held in the usual place, the dignified surroundings of the Senior Library, but in a squalid and revolting changing-room adjoining the gymnasium in the Coronation Wing.

There was a general rush of fuming Ribbons towards this degrading place in the hope of being able to hold a short indignation-meeting before Mother Peagle came. But such hopes were dashed, for there, seated on a decrepit old chair, with Prudence simpering beside her, was Mother Peagle ahead of them, and motioning them all to squat on the floor.

Mother Peagle began at once, oracular behind her spectacles.

'Close the door. Thank you. Ahem —'

Every eye was fixed on her face.

'Don't stare so, children, or I shall never get through. I have a difficult task before me — the task of asking you to accept, and enforce upon others, a certain number of what you will feel to be irksome and unreasonable regulations, and without being able to offer even you Ribbons any explanation. From today, from now, the entire school will be confined to the Coronation Wing.'

She hurried on, acutely conscious of the almost incredulous hostility which her words excited.

Only one face suspended judgment; it was Verity's.

'No one may leave this wing without the permission of a nun. A Ribbon's permission is not enough. Meals will be served in the gymnasium. Classes will be held in the dormitories. I am afraid it is going to mean a good deal of discomfort and exceptionally hard work for you Ribbons.'

Only one voice was heard when Mother Peagle came to an uncomfortable pause. It was Prudence's.

'I am sure I am speaking for all here, Mother, if I say we have perfect trust in whatever Reverend Mother and you think best.'

'Thank you, Prudence.' But it was not the voice Mother Peagle wanted to hear.

Torquilla spoke in a voice of bitter politeness.

'I suppose it is no use asking any questions?'

'Not where the main facts are concerned, I fear, Torquilla.'

'It's a bit thick,' muttered Alauda.

'I was only going to ask,' Torquilla said, 'if the Ribbon tea-banquet which was to have been given to Verity this afternoon in the refectory must be given up? It would be only the Ribbons, and we could shorten the time. But — my mother has sent us the cake.'

There was a kind of gasp: Torquilla's mother's cakes were about a yard in diameter and quite two inches thick in icing and cream.

Torquilla stood, scorning to plead for the tea-banquet.

Mother Peagle knew that it would be added insult to suggest that the tea-banquet might be given in the Coronation Wing.

'Oh well,' she said hurriedly. 'If the

cake has been made — if you all keep together in the refectory, and are not too long — I should hate to deprive Verity of her celebration.'

'Does that mean, yes, Mother?'

'Oh, I — I think so, Torquilla.'

'Thank you, Mother.'

But there was no warmth, no applause.

The meeting broke up, each member setting off at once on her disgusting task of spreading the news and herding the victims to the hated Coronation Wing.

17

Olive and Oliver

'Olive —'

'Yes, Super?'

The Superintendent of Police at Harrington has not yet been introduced except as heartily endorsing Sergeant Baseldon's plan for giving Olive a chance, but he existed, and his name, by a coincidence, was Oliver — Oliver Austin. He was youngish to have gained his rank, but had entered the Force by way of the Police College, where he had done extremely well. At thirty-four he was a man whom even Sergeant Baseldon, apt to be highly critical of men, approved, liked and even admired.

Olive, when not in a 'mood', could never be sufficiently thankful for an appointment which had given her the Sergeant and his 'Missus' for loving friends, and 'Super' Oliver Austin for her superior officer. It is something when a young woman in employment receives every consideration and never hears an impatient or harsh word. In return she had brought her womanly arts to work on the station, which thus had pretty curtains at its windows, and in season window-boxes, was dusted as no char would have dusted, and its many grim-looking books and papers kept in order.

On this morning of depression and fog the Super, on arrival at the station, had received one of those telephone calls which ask, is it you, and then tell you to hold on please. Such calls are apt to raise a little pleasurable excitement inasmuch as they often come from the big shots; and indeed the voice which took over from the secretary was none other than that of Sir Andrew Pearson, Deputy Commissioner of the Force.

Oliver Austin pricked up his ears.

He pricked up his ears even more when he heard, after a few kindly words, that he was to betake himself and as many officers as could be spared up to

Harrington Convent, where an important job of work was on hand. The Deputy himself was in charge, but Superintendent MacTavish was representing him on the spot.

'MacTavish will tell you all about it, and you will be his second-in-command. It's a big job, Austin,' said the Deputy, 'and it may be tricky and dangerous. It isn't because you happen to be at Harrington that I'm putting you on, but because you're the best man I know for it.'

'Very good of you to say so, sir.'

'Oh, and that reminds me. I should like to congratulate you on the very quick and competent handling of the Dump Case, which led to the discovery of those poison darts —'

'That was our Miss Churston, sir.'

'Olive Churston? Give her my very kind regards. I have not forgotten her handling of that handwriting case. What sort of a girl is she?'

'First-rate. I mean, sir, a very promising young officer.' He remembered in time to sound impersonal and official, but Sir

Andrew at his end smiled none the less.

And so Olive, on herself arriving at the station, was summoned into the Super's room.

'I say, Olive, we *are* going up in the world. That was the Deputy. There's some whale of a job at Harrington Convent —'

She nodded quickly.

' — and I'm to be third under himself and old MacTavish. He congratulated you no end on the Dump Case and sent his kindest regards. Actually asked what you were like —'

'And what did you say?'

'If I'd said the truth, the whole truth, and nothing but the truth, I shouldn't have got up to the Convent today. Olive, when are you going to put me out of my misery and say you'll marry me?'

'Oliver, I never met any man I liked as much as you. But — I don't know if I shall ever marry. I'm too moody. I'm not fit —'

'Dearest, if you like me — love would soon come. I'd make it. As for never marrying, don't talk such utter nonsense.

135

As for not being fit, don't hurt me, girl.'

'I certainly don't want to do that.'

'But it does. And so does this police business. It isn't *you* —'

'I — I don't know what is *me*. I — I sometimes think I should be happiest as a — nun —'

He looked at her with absolute horror.

'A — nun! You're not a Catholic —'

'People become Catholics.'

'Then do by all means, if you'd like. I would never say a word against what you want. But a nun — Olive —'

'You don't see that with some people — God has to come first?'

'Yes, I do. But don't beg the question.'

'What question?'

'Whether you are such a person.'

'You don't think so?'

'I am sure you want to put God first. But these aren't the Middle Ages, Olive. The 'world' is no longer classed with the flesh and the devil in quite the old easy-going way.'

'Easy-going?'

He pressed his point. 'It was taken for granted there was only one way to God.

136

But that idea is a back-number. An ugly word 'escapism' has cropped up —'

'Oliver. Of all things, nuns aren't 'escapists'.'

'I didn't say they were, dear. I only said that we now know there is such a thing.'

'You — you think I am one?'

'I didn't say that either.'

'What did you say? I'm all muddled up.'

'I said there was more than one way to God.'

'As if I didn't know that —'

He gave her a keen look, and went on. 'Olive, have you such a down on the world? After two wars it needs all the help it can get. Didn't God so love the world —?'

'That's quibbling. I should be working for it — praying for it —'

'Yes. But not living in it. Condescending to it.'

'You are unfair. I shouldn't —'

'This world,' he said quietly, 'this world, taken as a whole — not put away, but embraced, with all its duties and hardships and sufferings — and the love of God still kept foremost: isn't that the 'Valley of Soul-making' which Keats spoke about?'

'But what about the leaving all and following Him?'

'Christ spoke to the spirit,' he said. There was a pause, and he went on.

'It's no use arguing, dear. If you feel you must do this, then there is an end.' He got up and walked the room. 'I hadn't a notion —'

'I hadn't myself. It — it came suddenly — when I met the Reverend Mother up there —'

'I see.'

'You think it a fancy, Oliver? Perhaps it is. But I have always longed to — know how — to pray —'

'Yes. Well, I must be getting along.'

'Oliver, I'm not — certain — about anything —'

'No, dear. But I am. Remember that.'

'If I married anyone — Oliver, Oliver —'

'I am not giving you up, dearest.'

He took her very gently in his arms and kissed her. But not on the lips.

When he was gone her lips yearned,
and she cried.

18

Recalls a Famous Question
About Moses

The school, however — or, as Mr.
MacTavish called it, the 'Schule' — did
not take its removal to the Coronation
Wing so hard as the Ribbons did.
Children on the whole enjoy makeshift.
The Junior School was charmed, and the
Middle School hardly less, though it
dissembled its feelings more. Meals in
the gymnasium definitely stimulated
appetite, and there was immense curiosity to know how lessons in the
dormitories would be managed in view
of the cubicles. The question, Why all
this thusness? did not cross these
accommodating minds: *How*? was what
interested them. After all, the same sort
of thing occurred from time to time at
home, and was generally the builders, the
painters or the plumbers.

Bright and cheerful morning faces surrounded, therefore, the first *table d'hôte* in the gymnasium, and the fun was to see if you could do a little gymnasium without attracting the eye of a Ribbon.

'Silly little fools!' grumbled Alauda, and she dealt out impositions of cruel length. But Verity, now for the first time in exercise of authority, generally contrived to be looking another way.

'That's not the way to be a Ribbon,' Alauda informed her. So she caught the next offender and tickled her till she squealed.

Verity was easily the most popular Ribbon after that first breakfast, and yet it was found that in more serious matters the children obeyed her: to the annoyance of Alauda.

Prudence also protested against Verity's methods. 'It is no true kindness to be over-indulgent,' she said.

Torquilla requested both Alauda and Prudence to dry up. 'Recommend me to the blooming haristocracy and the 'unco guid' for downright cruelty to children,' she said. And she went on, to Verity:

'Don't forget the tea-banquet, Verity, old thing.'

'You bet I won't. When you give a tea, Torquilla, it *is* a tea.'

Torquilla looked sulky, as she always did when pleased. She actually took Verity's arm. After all, one did one's best, getting up tea-banquets and what-not: it was something to meet with a spot of real gratitude. Alauda was 'sounding brass' and Prudence was 'tinkling cymbal', but good old Verity, if you asked Torquilla, had the indispensable charity.

Which reminded Torquilla of something, and she ranged her lion-like way until she penned the harassed Mother Peagle into a corner.

'Wouldn't some other time do, dear?'

'It's nothing, Mother. Only I was beastly to you at the meeting this morning. I'm sorry and all that —'

Mother Peagle dropped all the numerous dry goods she had in her arms, the better to embrace Torquilla.

'My dear child — it makes just all the difference. I can manage anything if I know my Ribbons are supporting me —'

'Well, we are — 'specially Verity. Thanks about the tea-banquet, Mother; we'll do all you told us.'

'My dear, you have made me so very happy. God bless you.'

And Mother Peagle hurried away, dry goods and all, before the slight moisture of her eyes should become apparent to Torquilla.

The day became, if possible, darker and yellower, but nobody in the Coronation Wing cared. Lessons in the dormitories were a huge success, and all the mistresses in specially good tempers. Dinner in the gymnasium was eaten with twice the relish it had ever had in the handsome refectory. One got so sick of the refectory, with its dark wood and panels. Now, in the gymnasium you could look around and see the trapeze, the 'horse', and the ropes for climbing.

Nobody got the faintest inkling of the squads of police which kept on arriving at the back entrance and being directed to strategic points about the main buildings.

Nor, in the total black-out of the fog, did the police notice a large hooded lorry parked in a builder's clearance just up the Lane.

The natural darkness of an autumn evening was now thickening the already thrice-thickened darkness of the fog, and terror lurked, but in a corner of the School refectory was a table brilliant with electric lamps. This mysterious and tremendous force in one of its domesticated forms condescended to reveal the splendour of Torquilla's cake set forth for the occasion. There were also beautiful blooms stolen from the greenhouses. That is, Reverend Mother's permission for them had been obtained, but Mr. Turtle opposed an immovable refusal, so that Philomene had been obliged to purloin those issued for the altar, comforting her conscience with the thought that they would revert to their sanctified use after the tea-banquet.

Altogether, it was a pretty scene, and promptly at the hour named Torquilla took her place as hostess and received the Ribbons as if she had never set eyes on them before, Alauda also favouring the arrivals with an annihilating aristocratic stare.

Verity thoroughly understood her position as guest of honour. She lurked apart, keeping her eye on the refectory door and timing her own arrival for a full minute after all the bidden guests were assembled.

She was received with a great rattling of spoons in tea-cups. The Ribbon bosom was unanimous in being very glad to see her. Not only did the Ribbons feel more power to their elbows through her but they expected to be far better entertained than when Prudence, who was at that stage of a possible vocation which is an unmitigated nuisance to all less-favoured souls, had been apt to set the *tone*.

Torquilla was on her guard against this, and no sooner had the guest of honour been acclaimed than she gave the board a mighty thump and began to address the meeting.

'Welcome to Verity —'

'I am sure we are all very —' Prudence was beginning. But Torquilla shouted her down.

'I vote we leave the speeches until we've got outside the tea. Any objections?'

There was none.

'So I'll only say just now,' resumed Torquilla, 'that we're all very glad to have Verity with us. She has many faults —'

'Hear, hear!' from Alauda.

' — as we jolly well all have —'

'It is too true,' sighed Prudence.

' — but she isn't a drug on the market,' went on Torquilla, amid general agreement. 'So, Verity, consider yourself jolly well *persona grata*, as the Pope says. And now, if all you ladies are like-minded, what about —?'

'We haven't said grace yet,' admonished Prudence.

'*Benedictus benedicat*. Yes, we have,' said Torquilla; and plunging the knife into the cake, she helped herself to a large slice and handed on the plate to Verity on her right.

'Much obliged, Torquilla,' Verity said. 'I'll keep any little rejoinder I have to make to your kind words until later. At present, here's looking to you. In the words of the poet Byron, 'Let joy be unconfined'; that is, don't let's have any shop-talk while we're eating. Let me down gently. No religion and no politics, please.'

'O.K. by me,' mumbled Torquilla.

The cake went the round of the table.

No arrangements of any kind had been made for pouring out, and so nobody would have had anything to drink had not Philomene felt very thirsty and provided herself with a cup. It was then a case of *noblesse oblige*, and everybody was served, without any inquiries as to how they liked it: after which Philomene doused the tea-pot, remarking that if anyone wanted a second cup they could jolly well get up and help themselves.

Philomene returned to her place to find that a young and particularly innocent-looking Ribbon seated beside her, by name Angela Manners, had been thieving, and a disgraceful scene ensued which would have shocked the Junior School.

Otherwise, 'joy was unconfined'. Verity had brought a large box of crackers, and everybody was soon adorned with a paper-cap, some of which were very *à propos*, Torquilla having a mortar-board, Alauda a coronet, and Prudence a halo.

Half an hour later Verity arose amid applause to propose her own health and make the speech of the evening.

'Two minutes' silence, ladies, if you please, while we all reverently contemplate the excelling virtues of the Peaglums —'

Two minutes' loud and ribald din followed, and Verity resumed:

'Among other instances of famous conversions, I may suggest St. Paul on the Damascus road and Cardinal Newman seeing the face of a Monophysite in his shaving-glass.'

'What's a 'Monophysite'?' from Angela Manners.

'A theologian who bones cake. Go on, Verity.'

'But the conversion of the Peaglums, which has had the happy result of bringing me here among you this evening, is greater than these. It must indeed have been a *blinding* light which closed her eyes at last to the 'many faults' in your obedient servant to which our president,' with a bow to Torquilla, 'has made such happy allusion.'

Torquilla, gorged with cake, her mortar-board drooping over one eye, blinked much as a boa-constrictor might in similar circumstances, amiably.

There was gratifying outcry. 'Go on, Verity. Go on —'

And Verity did go on.

'And while, ladies, we are speaking of blinding lights —'

And there she suddenly broke off.

She stopped indeed, and that was as much of her speech as was ever uttered.

For all the lights went out.

19

Apparently the End of the World

The eclipse was total.

Packed together as they were, the Ribbons could yet see nothing of each other.

They knew they were in the refectory, but all sense of direction was gone from them.

Where, for example, was the door?

Startled silence reigned. But then the voice of Torquilla was heard, sounding as from far away.

'Only a bust fuse. Sit tight. It'll soon come on again. Anyone got a match?'

''Hellish dark and smells of cheese —'' quoted Verity. 'Yes, I've got a box — I think —'

She was felt to be feeling all over herself.

'You don't have to be modest,' Alauda said: to which Prudence duly objected.

'Here it is, and — dash! — there's only three in it. What do you think, Torquilla? Shall I light one now, so we can see where the door is? If this is general, we ought to be being useful.'

'The wing has its own plant,' someone said. 'They'll be all right up there.'

'Yes, but do let's have a match.' So said several voices, from which a quiver was not altogether absent.

'Funny everything's so quiet. I can't hear a sound.'

'It's no use lighting a match,' Verity said, 'unless we know exactly what we're going to do while the light lasts. Here's what I suggest —'

She was interrupted by a voice definitely bordering on hysteria. 'I — I can't breathe. I don't believe it is a fuse.'

'Of course not,' Alauda said, 'it's the end of the world. The Day of Judgment will follow shortly —'

An invisible elbow shot out and caught Alauda in the ribs. It was Torquilla's elbow.

'Shut up. Everybody shut up. Now then, Verity, what were you going to say?'

151

'While the match is burning we all catch hold of each other behind Torquilla, and then follow-my-leader to the door.'

'Sound scheme. Ready with the match?'

Verity struck. But the stick broke short in her hand, and in the meagre ray which flickered for a second stampede prevailed. There were scuffles, falls, and a scream. The flame was upon Verity's very fingers before any concerted move could be made.

'Stay where you are,' Verity cried, and immediately struck another match. This one burnt clear, but its light was too dim for so large a space, and before much use could be made of it to restore order there was a terrific *thud* somewhere in the distance, followed by a concussion of the floor — and a sudden violent draught blowing into the room extinguished the flame, leaving the Ribbons in worse plight than before.

Torquilla's voice was immediately raised, but if panic was averted at that moment it was owing to Verity, who came forward with a suggestion which might be held to explain things.

'I know what it is. It's an earthquake! Only a little one of course, but a definite earthquake. Don't you think so, Torquilla?'

'That's what it was,' affirmed Torquilla, with a confidence she was far from feeling.

'It was a fuse last time,' said Alauda.

'And it'll be your head next time,' said Torquilla.

'Don't you think it would be a good thing,' said the voice of Prudence, 'if we all said the Rosary?'

'Any takers for that?' inquired Torquilla.

Nobody spoke; so Prudence, with a sigh, set to work on the exercise alone.

She was instantly rewarded: a light appeared in the room.

It was not exactly a reassuring light, being fulvous and lambent, but it was a light, and revealed the Ribbons to one another again, so that all began setting clothes to rights and adjusting less than elegant poses. Alauda, having a Norman nose, was the first to detect the nasty smell which seemed to come with the light, and nobody could help hearing the sounds of hurrying footsteps, muffled voices, and, as it seemed to the Ribbons, from somewhere far away the shrill screams of children.

Verity was the first to react. 'Let's get out. 'I hear the sound of voices calling —''

''Poor old Jo'!' said Torquilla. 'Yes, let's get out. But all together. I'll lead the way — with you, Verity, and you, Alauda. Muriel, you next, with Celia, Tiphaine, Eileen, Kathryn, Barbara. Prudence, will you take charge of the rearguard, with Phil, Jamette, Angela, Joan, Gill, Teresa, Valerie and Rosemary. That's right. Come along.'

The formation passed out through the door and into the corridor. The smell became worse and blew against them in warm gusts with a weakening, disheartening effect. They all felt as if they were toiling up a steep hill. The light grew brighter and more yellow; there was smoke and what sounded like the crackling of fire. The ranks exchanged questioning glances and wavered, but Torquilla, Verity and Alauda still led on.

They went very slowly, because their legs and arms were heavy, and they did not speak, because they needed all their breath to breathe with. Signs of collapse were definitely beginning to appear.

And somehow they could not find their way back to the Coronation Wing.

It was at a certain point, when even Torquilla was conscious of failing powers, that they were overtaken by a stout gentleman in a great hurry. He drew up beside them, and seemed of such immense strength that they were all somehow able to lean against him while they fetched a deeper breath.

'Och, noo, ma puir bonny lasses,' he exhorted them, 'ye'll sune be there. Come awa' noo, and let me into the midst of ye. That's the gir-r-ls! Noo I can be the ingine and give ye a whir-r-l along.'

He was better than his word. Not only did he 'whirl' the whole exhausted Ribbonhood along, but he infallibly detected the ones nearest fainting and carried them. The fear of having this happen to her was sufficient to keep Prudence, who took the most Aloysian views of purity, on her tottering feet.

Next minute they were all in the Coronation Wing again, breathing pure air with gasps and sobs and sighs of relief. The strange man was gone, but hurrying towards them with arms outstretched as if to embrace them all and with exclamations of affectionate concern came Mother Peagle, and there was a sufficient revival of strength to enable one and all to exclaim with united breath:

'*The Peaglums!*'

20

The 'Brainwave' of Thistle Macbinkie

One mystery at any rate explained itself to the Ribbons as they subsided upon the chairs or even on the floor of the room into which Mother Peagle took them. That distant sound of screams which they had heard from below certainly did not mean that the School was being killed off like so many little piglets. Mother Peagle would hardly have maintained her composure if a Massacre of the Innocents were going on next door.

Yet the screaming was much louder up here, and it definitely was screaming. But above its shrillness sounded the piano under the ever-obliging hands of Mother Frederica, and her tunes were of the gayest, and the screamers were also frantically dancing, and bursting into fits of laughter and falling down on the floor.

It was indeed a case of 'revelry by

night', but there was no sign of 'The foe! they come! they come!', for those who would ordinarily have been the foe of such goings-on — i.e. the nuns — could be heard actually taking part.

Beyond a point the brain will not function. The Ribbons could only direct a 'wild surmise' at Mother Peagle.

She did look a little ashamed of herself.

'You are wondering what all the noise is about? Well, one does not as a rule have a party on a Vigil, and tonight is the Vigil of All Saints. But the children have been so good all day, and it has been a little dull for them, so when little Thistle MacBinkie told Reverend Mother that in Scotland the Vigil of All Saints is called 'Hallowe'en', and they always have parties on it, she said they could have a party — a Scots party. First we had dressing-up, and charades, and then Mr. MacTavish — that was the gentle-man you met — came and danced the Highland fling. My dear, you would never have thought he could, but he seems a most expert performer; it was really beautiful. And then, when he had to go away, Thistle took over, and they have all been dancing Highland reels and quadrilles ever since. Apparently you always scream when you dance in Scotland, and of course that appealed to the children immensely. I don't know when they have enjoyed themselves so much. And it came in so handy. Really God is very good. None of them has a notion anything has been happening. Well, well, I must be getting back. We are but poorly staffed. If any of you Ribbons feel equal to it later on I wish —'

'I feel equal to it now, Mother,' Verity said. 'I love quadrilles —'

Jamette was still really ill, and rather disgraced her Ribbonhood by crying and refusing to go to bed unless Torquilla took her. Torquilla therefore went off with her, promising to come along as soon as she could. Muriel and some others volunteered, but were rejected by Mother Peagle as still too groggy. 'What about you, Alauda?' Mother Peagle said.

Alauda had never had an ache or a pain in her life and was equal to almost any endurance. She was at the moment as fit as a fiddle, but she contrived to look fiddle-faced. 'I'll come, too, later on,' she said, 'but at present I still feel a bit —By the way, Mother, you haven't told us a thing yet about the air — or the bang we heard — or about the fire —'

But Mother Peagle had bustled out of the room in one of those sudden great hurries of hers. Verity was waiting for her outside. Torquilla returned with good news of Jamette, who was fast asleep. Though really very tired, Torquilla at once squared her shoulders for the next duty. Neither of the girls asked any questions, although they had Mother Peagle for a moment to themselves: it was Mother Peagle who in a low voice volunteered a little information.

'You have probably guessed that all this has something to do with — Inez? You know that attempts have been made on her life by revolutionists from her own country — where matters are, I fear, in a sad state. This evening the whole Convent was attacked — with quick-firing guns and some sort of stupefying gas — and actually a small bomb was exploded in, of all places, the chapel — and fire broke out —'

'It is still burning,' Verity cried. 'We heard it and saw it. Oh, Mother, couldn't we help?'

'My dear child, we could on no account risk any of you children. Thank God you are all safe —'

'Inez?' Torquilla said.

'Inez too — and the police hope they have the matter in hand. And you Ribbons — God be for ever thanked and praised. I could not think what had become of you. I totally forgot about the tea-banquet. If you could know what I felt when I saw you — my poor children. I cannot say what I think of your discipline and courage —'

'We thought it was a bust fuse,' muttered Torquilla, with one of her fierce blinks aside — at Verity, as much as to say, 'Do nothing to encourage the Peaglums in this maudlin vein and, if you can, think of some way of heading her off.'

Verity rose to the occasion.

'What a splendid idea to have a party,

Mother. Shall we go in? That music makes my toes tickle. I'm simply dying to be dancing.'

It was Mother Peagle's turn to bestow a look, and her look was not so easily to be interpreted as Torquilla's. It certainly was not a look of reproach. It was, had Verity known, a look of sheer gratitude. Mother Peagle had had a gruelling day, in constant anxiety for the very lives of other people's children. This brunt she had borne practically alone, her superiors preoccupied, her juniors hardly realizing. Now she was utterly tired out. But there was a sweetness in her heart, for she had found in the high spirit and alacrity of Verity's words something which definitely cheered her up.

21

The Battle of Harrington

(IN SIX PARTS)

1. WHY SUPPRESSED IN THE NEWS

The Battle of Harrington would have been a nine-days' wonder indeed but for the fact that the Government, acting on the advice of the police, suppressed all report of it.

The police thought it not in the interests of the public that the facts should be made known.

The Government agreed with the police. The Home Secretary was approached, who called in his colleague for Foreign Affairs; and together they interviewed the Prime Minister.

The Prime Minister called a meeting of the Press, and after stating the facts of Harrington to the great owners and editors he asked them to accept the ruling of the Government that it was not in the interests of the public to make such facts known.

In a democratic country the Press, provided its privileges are considered, is always ready to cooperate with the Government; and thus, though many thousands of people were soon in the secret, they kept their mouths closed, and no newspaper 'carried', as the expression is, a report of what took place at Harrington on the night of the 31st October 19 — .

Thus the Lady Gale, who was at the Italian Lakes at the time, saw nothing in her *Continental Daily Mail* to give her the least alarm for the tender and Honourable Alauda, and the money she would certainly have spent on jet-transport remained in her pocket.

Thus the MacBinkie of MacBinkie perused his Sassenach journal with no more than his usual indignation that there should be no word in it of the crying wrongs of Scotland, and sat down at once to write a long letter to the *Scotsman* demanding that the Queen be known as Queen Elspeth, Elspie or Tibby.

2. HOW CONNECTED WITH THE LATE 'MR. SMITH'

It is more than probable that had 'Mr. Smith — of Birmingham' lived, the Battle of Harrington would never have taken place.

'Mr. Smith', as his luggage suggested, was a man of devious and subtle approaches. He had also an intense respect for his own skin. He was the leader and mastermind of those enthusiastic young Anacondans who came to England charged with the liquidation of Inez. There is some reason for believing that, but for certain circumstances which he did not foresee, he would have accomplished his purpose. But the circumstances arose, he became too soon what Mrs. Parsley called a 'corp', and the leadership which was his devolved upon others.

These others were not like 'Mr. Smith'.

They were hot-heads. In a heyday of revolvers, tommy-guns and what-have-you, they had no time for such methods as poison darts. Nor was it with them now just a matter of liquidating an Escapado, it was a matter also of taking terrible revenge for 'Mr. Smith'. It would do these nuns no harm to be shown the consequences of murdering a 'Smith' and sheltering an Escapado.

The fog put heart in them. For the police they felt contempt — an unarmed force! Recruiting added two young Oriental thugs to their number, and some ex-alumni of 'approved' schools rallied to the cause. Probably a dozen men took part in the attack on the Convent. It was a well-planned attack, based on the researches of that late 'student' 'Mr. Smith', who in one bogus capacity or another had several times contrived to get inside.

Anacondans, through living so much in the jungle, have developed some faculties not possessed in the same degree by others. They can climb like monkeys. They can see in the dark. They are thoroughgoing. The new leader, though he lacked the subtlety of 'Mr. Smith', had neglected nothing.

Thus the swooping invaders were fearful and wonderful to behold. Each man wore the full kit of a motor-cyclist snouted with a gas-helmet. They were armed with revolvers and tommy-guns. They had several cylinders of a stupefying gas, also incendiary bombs, and one small high-explosive bomb.

They had upon their persons every known contrivance for making weird and terrifying noises. They could shriek and mutter and groan.

3. STRATEGY AND TACTICS

The frontal attack — that is, on Mother Peck's door — was made in silence by three men.

They crept up and blew it off its hinges with hand-grenades. They poured in the fire of tommy-guns, from which the police withdrew; and then, with indescribable shrieks and howls, they themselves rushed into the porch, their guns still directed upon the police.

But they had overlooked one factor, as had the police likewise — and that factor was Mother Peck.

Mother Peck was not going to be dislodged from her rightful place by what was obviously a gang of young toughs made up for Guy Fawkes' Day. Arming herself with a huge black ruler, without which she never ruled the smallest line, she rushed upon the intruders with flying veil and beat down the muzzles of their guns.

'This is *too* much. What do you *mean* by such conduct? A gang of great naughty boys trying to frighten people! You ought to be birched —'

The police rushed to her assistance, and in the scrimmage Mother Peck was borne to the ground. But, if down, she was by no means out. She still had the great ruler, and with this she 'tackled low'.

Two of the young men got away, but the third had his shin half cracked by the ruler and was glad to be rescued by the police, who took him into custody.

At the same time as the frontal attack the Convent was entered at two other points: by seven men at the back entrance, and by two through a chute into the basement.

The two had, so to speak, a roving commission of damage. It was they who fused all the lights — indeed, actually sabotaged the plant. They burst all the boilers they came across and tore up all telephone installations by the roots. The great kitchen with all its labour-saving devices they so systematically devastated that when they had finished not even an egg could have been boiled there.

When a force of police got on their tracks they gave it a good peppering with their tommy-guns and left it to survey the ruins while themselves rushed off to rejoin the main body.

The larger contingent, which entered at the back, encountered only a ninety-year-old Bretonne lay-sister, more than half blind, and at that moment occupied with the Glorious Mystery of the Coronation of Our Lady in Heaven. To the dim sight and pious absorption of this dear old woman the 'Comrades' appeared as probably some plumbers or gas-fitters arriving, weeks behind time, on some urgent work of repair; and with fervent thanks to the Holy Mother, who, though crowned by the Almighty in everlasting bliss, could still spare a thought for the Convent's humbler needs, she smiled with seraphic toothlessness and sped the 'plumbers' with a blessing on their way.

Their way led straight to the Convent chapel!

Now the Comrades were in a hurry; it was tip and run for them. But they were high-minded young men and, confronted with Superstition, felt a duty to society. Besides, a moment would suffice to time a fuse — to scatter some incendiaries. All these rich carpets and curtains would do the rest.

Quickly they fell to work.

Their work done, they rushed on and out into the cloister, where they found, drawn up and with tommy-guns in position, all the other Comrades — all, that is, but the one captured by Mother

Peck. There was just time for the Red fist-shake, a bar or two of the 'Red Flag'. Then, under a furious bombardment of all eleven tommy-guns, the Comrades charged in the direction of the infirmary, the police retiring before them.

It was the Supreme Moment for the Comrades. The Convent lay helpless at their mercy.

4. REVEREND MOTHER SAVES THE BLESSED SACRAMENT

The police, taking cover behind doors, watched the triumphant charge of the Comrades with approval. Let the perishers round 'emselves up. The police asked nothing better.

Superintendent MacTavish whistled the 'March of the Cameron Men'.

'It's a peety,' he said, 'they havena the pipes.' He then looked pawkier, if possible, than usual, and delivered himself to Oliver Austin in a series of proverbs.

'Have ye ever heard tell, Mr. Austin,

what it is that gangs before a fall? Ye'll have heard the auld Roman adage to the effect *Quem Deus vult perdere prius dementat?* They've exposed their flank, the loons. And if yon Reverend Mother body hadn't told me to risk no police lives I've an idea I could settle with 'um,'

'She said that, did she?' Oliver answered. Since his conversation with Olive he had taken a great prejudice against Reverend Mother. Taking advantage of a young girl — wasn't that what nuns were always doing? Still, he thought it was nice of Reverend Mother to feel for police lives. And, by Jove, these women were plucky.

No one had a notion as yet that the Comrades had left a surprise-packet in the chapel; and thus Mother Vannes, the sacristan, slipping in to have a look round, was blown violently out again and stretched on her back in the cloister half choked with smoke and flame.

'Dear me —' was all she had time for as she lost consciousness.

But a bomb announces itself. Nuns now came running from all quarters. Also police. Reverend Mother was there at once. Mother Assistant a second later. MacTavish was hot on their heels.

Smoke and bright yellow flame was pouring through the entrance.

'Don't ye noo, Reverend Leddyship. Woman, have sense.'

Thus MacTavish, crying hoarsely, and actually detaining Reverend Mother by the sleeve. 'Wait noo, ma bonny leddy, till my men have —'

Reverend Mother gently freed herself and with a perfectly expressionless face passed through the flame and up the steps of the altar.

Mother Assistant immediately followed.

'Hech, sirs — hech, sirs! Noo when did a body see the like. Daft they are — sheer daft. If the Lord doesna juist repeat the miracle of Shadrach, Meshach and Abednego I'm sure I dinna ken what's to become of the poor dear doited reverend ladies —'

At this point in his lamentations the Superintendent was interrupted by the reappearance of Reverend Mother clasping under her veil the ciborium containing the Blessed Sacrament which she had rescued from the Tabernacle, and almost immediately after her came Mother Assistant carrying the door of the Tabernacle, a heavy sheet of gold encrusted with gems gifted to the Convent, which she had by sheer manual strength wrenched from its hinges.

Neither of the two seemed to have suffered scathe in the fiery interlude, and MacTavish would have thrown himself upon them in congratulations when he realized in time that Reverend Mother must by no means be spoken to at present. She stood holding the ciborium while the other nuns knelt worshipping around her, even Mother Vannes recovering consciousness in time to stretch out her arms. No heed at all was paid to the valuable door, but it was just set on one side. A procession was formed behind Reverend Mother, a bell tinkled and a psalm was raised, and she led at a slow pace, with eyes withdrawn in ecstasy, along the corridors to the New Building, where in an improvised chapel the snowy-headed novices and their mistress received the Elements with adoration.

MacTavish wept to see them go, and declared ever after that if he hadna been a Presbyterian he would juist have joined the Auld Kirk.

5. TRIUMPH OF POLICE AND NUNS

While they were gone a strong body of police under Oliver Austin also broke through the flames and began beating them down as best they could. With the telephones cut there was no sending for engines, and though police were dispatched on motor-cycles they had to go very slow in the whirl and smother of the fog.

Reverend Mother, Mother Assistant and many other nuns were soon back from the New Building and joined the police in the fray against the fire.

MacTavish meanwhile went off with Oliver Austin to inquire what news there was of the Comrades. They were told that at first there had been furious whoopee, but it had died down, and now for a long time nothing had been heard.

MacTavish in a loud voice summoned them to surrender. 'Noo then, you lads up there, you've had your bit of fun, but noo the game is up. What about coming quietly?'

There was no reply. The Comrades, though seeming all for quietness, obeyed the summons in no other way.

'Foxing, sir, if you ask me,' said a sergeant.

'Foxing? I'll fox 'em!' And MacTavish and Austin began mounting the stairs.

'Mind your eyes, gentlemen. They were shootin' not so long ago.'

'Hoot awa'. You're not a married man, are ye, Austin?'

'No, sir,' said Oliver with a pang.

'And ma wife has got grown-up sons and daughties.' He broke off to address three magnificent young sergeants who were also on the stairs.

'Noo then, what do you wee laddies think you're doing? Fine I ken you're all married men with weans. Oot of it with all three o' ye, or am I to report ye for insubordination? What would her Reverend Leddyship say if she saw ye trying to shirk the duties of paternity?'

The sergeants merely grinned and looked stolid.

'Aweel. Wha wull to Cupar maun to Cupar. Keep ye well ahint, and don't show your thick heads till me and Mr. Austin has had ours took off us.'

Those words of Mr. MacTavish's might well have been his last, for his next step brought him onto the landing, which was exposed to the cross-fire of eleven tommy-guns and as many revolvers.

Oliver took the same step with him, and the sergeants followed in strict order of seniority.

The immediate result in all five was an outburst of sneezing and coughing.

'Ugh, ugh, ugh! Where are the blighters?' Oliver was gasping.

It was MacTavish who next found a voice — as a result of a particularly rending sneeze which must have cleared his passages.

'Come awa' noo, laddies. I am a police officer, and I arrest ye all on a charge of feloniously entering a dwelling-house with intent to wound and kill, and it's my duty to warn ye forby that anything ye say may be took doon in writing and used against ye —'

But he broke off, for a young sergeant was pointing with horror at what looked in the glare of the police-lamps like a number of enormous blackbeetles heaving leggily in a heap on the floor.

It was the Comrades.

The tale told itself. They had meant to use gas against the police before shooting their way down as they had shot it up. But they were inexpert in opening the cylinder, which proved refractory: someone had lost his nerve: panic ensued: weapons were thrown down, kit torn off, gas-masks dislodged. Now the suffocating Comrades were making a final struggle against the coma which assailed them.

Under artificial respiration applied downstairs the Comrades revived and sat sulkily round in No. 17 Parlour. Under interrogation they said they desired only the English Tower and the English Block.

They could also do with an English cup of tea — provided no English poison were put into it.

The tea (without poison) was served them at once, but they looked so miserable as they drank that the kindly MacTavish could not refrain from words of comfort.

'Hoot, toot, laddies. Dinna be too doon. Ye winna be hangit. Ye havena kill't anny-body.'

Not killed anybody! It was too much.

The English weather suddenly changing, the dense black English fog was somewhat cleared away, and Sir Andrew Pearson arrived. After a word with Mr. MacTavish, he drove on to the station, where he received an astonishing communication from Olive Churston.

The communication was amazing beyond words, and necessitated his immediate return to the Convent, where he also took Olive.

But he used the station telephone (undamaged) to make arrangements with a sitting magistrate, and so the Comrades were able to get through the formalities that night and sleep comfortably in Brixton.

6. ARRIVAL OF FR. WITHERSTICK

Mother Peagle was just wondering how in the world to deal with the riot set afoot by Thistle MacBinkie when Fr. Witherstick massively arrived.

Characteristically he knew nothing of the day's doings, and on being told by Mother Peagle he characteristically said nothing.

He proceeded at once to give Benediction, which caused all the little Bacchantes to put on veils and turn into little angels.

The ceremony over, Torquilla, Verity, Muriel and a few other Ribbons contrived by excellent staff-work that the only way open to the retiring worshippers was one which led straight to bed.

22

'But What Far Grove — '

No sooner was the Battle of Harrington over and won — for a battle must be said to be won when the enemy is incapable of further resistance — than Reverend Mother lost not a minute in going to the New Building to make sure that all was well with Inez.

She had little or even no doubt, for the Comrades had never got near the New Building; but she did feel that the whole thing must have been a terrible ordeal to the child, lying there and not knowing exactly what was happening.

She remembered, too, that Inez had, in spite of the kindness of Sir Andrew, a strange dislike of the police. Nothing could persuade her that they were on her side.

Reverend Mother's orders with regard to Inez during the course of the disturbance had been that a nun was to be in the bedroom with the child — it was to be a choir-nun, not a lay-sister; and Reverend Mother had been careful to choose a favourite of Inez's. Immediately outside the door were, of course, the two special detectives, and they were armed. Thus the only way of getting in upon Inez would have to be by the window, which was high from the ground, not very near any trees, and was to be kept shuttered until after the 'All Clear'.

If anybody was to kill or abduct Inez he would first have to perform the almost impossible feat of reaching the window-ledge from the trees, and there, hanging on by his hands, undo the shutter in the face of the armed opposition of two experienced detectives.

It is small wonder that Reverend Mother felt little anxiety as she hastened to the New Building with news which she hoped would put an end for ever to the child's suffering and terror. Not only were the Comrades all made prisoner, but that morning's *Times* had contained a very encouraging report from Anaconda.

Not for one moment that Reverend Mother sympathized with dictators or desired to see their triumph anywhere, but she certainly did feel that Don Magnifiguo, who was in some strange way a man of religious principles and, if a tyrant, on the benevolent side, was much to be preferred to the sheer anarchy and hatred which was contending with him. Therefore she could not be really sorry to read the following short paragraph:

'Even Communist sources admit that Don Magnifiguo, the Hazh Bazh, has inflicted a heavy defeat upon them in the jungle and has retaken the capital city of Lilitha. The people received him with acclamation, and he granted a general amnesty to all but foreign Communists. The rumour that he has declared Anaconda a republic with himself as interim President has not as yet been confirmed.'

None the less, the 'amnesty' warmed Reverend Mother's heart, and she decided to ring up her friend Sir Clement de Willowby without loss of time.

Thank God Inez was safe, for her father would be wanting news of her at once.

Reverend Mother was not anxious — it was absurd to be anxious when all was well: but she hurried, all the same.

She was almost running when she entered the New Building.

The sweet sound of the novices singing before the Blessed Sacrament came to her ears, and she would certainly have gone in but for a feeling that she must not delay just now.

She shook herself inwardly for such weakness, but she went quickly upstairs.

At the slightest sound the detectives were both out in the passage, but saluted and relaxed smiling, when they saw who came.

'All perfectly O.K., Your Reverence. The lady is still with the little girl. There hasn't been a sound.'

Reverend Mother never forgot her feelings when she opened the door. The room was in darkness. A great waft of cold air struck her full in the face from the window, which was unshuttered and thrown wide open.

A groan from something on the floor drew her attention, and for a frightful second she thought it was Inez — Inez stabbed, wounded, dying —

But it was not Inez. It was Sister Ursula stretched unconscious by the bed.

The two detectives were in the room, flooding every corner with light.

But the strong lights showed nothing.

It seemed as if the girl must have taken unto herself wings and flown from the room.

Inez was gone.

23

The Face in the Fog

All through that long day of fog and loneliness and lack of news Olive felt how stupidly true it is that 'men must work, and women must weep'.

Why should she not have gone to the Convent instead of being left to fiddle away her time at the station. Why make the pretence of having women police officers if the minute any crisis occurred they were to be discounted? How like *men* the whole thing was, always taking refuge against the competition of women by their so-called 'chivalry'!

Look at all the old stories from time immemorial. There was always a 'noble knight' who rescued (and usually married) some insipid but more than earthly beautiful 'princess' who got herself into trouble with a 'dragon' or other monster. It was never the noble knight who got into trouble and had to be rescued by the wit of the princess — though history teemed with instances of woman having to come to the aid of man.

As the day lengthened and the fog darkened and Olive felt more and more disconsolate she thought of Oliver, who was just like other men. He thought it only natural that she should share his life but was knocked all of a heap at the idea of her wanting a life of her own. She tried hard to feel more and more attracted to the life of a nun just to pay Oliver out, but it was no use: just as you could not marry unless you were really in love, so you could not become a nun unless you had that *something* which they had.

So the day passed by for Olive, and she lived like a bird on very small scraps of this and that, always with a cup of tea, and she longed for company and waged inner war with herself.

She wondered if anything was happening at the Convent, and if that poor child were in any danger, and if the nuns — and if Oliver —

And while she was considering this last

point with special intensity, suddenly she heard the *boom* of the explosion in the chapel.

What in all the world was that?

She had tried again and again to get through to the Convent on the telephone afterwards, becoming more and more alarmed when she continued to fail. In the end, unable to bear the inaction any longer, she decided to go out — not far — no farther than the bus terminus, where the shops might give a glimmer of light.

But, once outside, how quickly the station was swallowed away behind her, lights and all. She realized that just getting to the shops might be a task beyond her. The fog took away her breath and bewildered her: even her powerful lamp was baffled by it. The only way to get along was to grope — to grope from house to house.

Such going was very slow, and she stumbled incessantly. She was beset with what has been called the 'innate malice of inanimate objects'. Every doorstep was a man-trap; and when, exhausted by this stumbling, fumbling course, she ventured to steer out, up rose a lamp-post and knocked her spinning.

Believing herself attacked, she struck out, scrambled up and backed away, only to trip over the opposite kerb and take a header into a ditch.

Something seized her by the throat; fighting the horror off, she found it to be a great jagged arm of bramble.

She was now without any sense of direction at all. She did not know she had crossed the road. She was unnerved by disaster and in pain from the lamp-post's blow. Her nose was bleeding and her mouth full of blood. The bramble had lacerated her hand.

Climbing out of the ditch, she set forward again, now on hands and knees, and, as good luck would have it, she crossed the road again, moving diagonally. After what seemed an endless time she came to a place where the fog was thinner, and she saw the dim lights of the row of small shops which she knew to be exactly opposite the Harrington Hotel. Immense relief filled her; she at least knew where she was again, and ought to be able to crawl back to the station.

She sat down on the kerb for a while, cheered by the brightening lights of the shops. Was the fog clearing? It had receded from the pavement, and she thought there were rifts in it beyond.

There was one rift, if rift it was, which seemed to her especially promising, and she fixed her eyes on it. The fog deadened sound, nothing was to be heard as of a footstep, but as she gazed she saw to her amazement *a face pass by somewhere high up in the rift.*

Now was the time for Olive's lamp. But she had lost it; it must have fallen from her in the ditch. But she did not need it; the glimmer of the shops was sufficient, and for an instant before it was again eclipsed a face was revealed —

The beautiful face of Inez Escapado!

But again swooped the fog, obliterating everything.

24

Olive in Conference

Olive had to wait a long time before another lull in the fog occurred. It was only at long last that she was able to set off at a crawl, guiding herself with her hands, back to the station. Then she overshot the mark, had to think it all out again.

She was very much exhausted when she did at last arrive.

She had scarcely been indoors five minutes when, to her intense relief, Sir Andrew arrived, and she was able to pour out her story to him.

When he had done his telephoning about the magistrate he placed a chair for Olive and asked if he might have a private word with her before they returned to the Convent.

'You see, Miss — er — Olive, you were the first detective to — ah — investigate certain matters, and I think it very unlikely that you have not come to a few — er — tentative conclusions of your own.'

Olive, a low-grade and very junior detective officer, flushed a bright pink at being actually taken into conference with the Deputy Commissioner.

'I did. One can't help oneself. I expect I was all wrong.'

'As you say, one cannot help oneself. Did you, for instance, when you found the poison darts in the possession of the man 'Smith', suspect that an attempt had already been made upon the little girl, and that — someone — had shot him to prevent him?'

'Yes, Sir Andrew. And I felt pretty sure the man who — did the shooting — was this Juan Copanza.'

'The — er — Spanish gardener-man?'

'Yes. But then I had another idea, Sir Andrew —'

'Please tell me.'

'I know it sounds wild, but when the little girl was delirious she cried upon someone called Diego —'

'She did,' said Sir Andrew.

'Well, it occurred to me there was a secret, which sometimes she remembered and sometimes did not. And I wondered if perhaps Copanza and this Diego might perhaps be the same person —'

'That is — ah — profoundly interesting. Suggestive, one might say. Please go on, Miss — er — Olive.'

'The rest is pure guesswork —'

'Hypothesis,' murmured Sir Andrew.

'Well, I — got a feeling — that not Copanza but Diego was the real man, and — that — perhaps he was the — agent of — Inez's friends. Perhaps that explains,' Olive went on, 'why she hated the police —'

'Why?'

'Because she thought the police would arrest Diego for killing 'Smith', and then she would have no friend left to look after her. She couldn't be expected to know about 'justifiable homicide' — could she?'

Sir Andrew shook his head and seemed to pass into a kind of reverie.

'So your belief is,' he said at length,

'that Inez has gone off with this — Diego?'

'That's what I really do think —'

'Where has he been all this time? How did he keep in touch with the child?'

'I don't know the first answer now, but — I think I could tell you first thing after breakfast tomorrow morning — and — and perhaps some other things too. As for keeping in touch — he — he did it by sounds — sounds like a bird's — which Inez would understand, but nobody else. Then, though I hate to say it, I think they've had an accomplice inside the house.'

'This Sister Ursula?' said Sir Andrew.

'I suppose she'll get into very hot water, poor thing. But I'm perfectly sure she meant nothing but well. Please, Sir Andrew, ask Reverend Mother not to be too down on her.'

'I will make a note of it. But now, Miss — er — Olive, has this very astute mind of yours got as far as *where* these young people are likely to have gone?'

Olive shook her head. 'No. But I think if we all put our wits together — and get

Inez's friends in the School to remember things she may have said — I don't know a thing about Diego, not a thing, but I've a feeling a place chosen by him won't be too obviously on the map.'

'I suppose,' said Sir Andrew, 'we must advertise their descriptions in all parts?'

'I doubt if they'll answer those descriptions by tomorrow,' Olive said. 'Inez had on the queerest little bonnet which made it quite a job to recognize her.'

'In fact, my dear Miss Olive, are you sure you did recognize her? Or may she not have been some quite different child?'

Olive was almost cross.

'Oh well, if that's what you think of me —'

'I think very highly of you, my dear. So what we want now,' said Sir Andrew, 'is an answer to a question about a thing which is animal, vegetable and abstract.'

25

Mr. Turtle Rises to Heights
and Falls to Effect

Immediately after breakfast on the following morning Olive was off upon those further investigations which she had promised Sir Andrew.

Her way took her through the shrubberies into the kitchen gardens and to the Copanza-Diego hut.

As she passed through the shrubberies, however, she paused and looked back where, across the Lane, the bedroom windows of the Parsley house could be seen, plainly affording a view of where she stood.

Taking the greatest care not to kneel or contact the ground with her hands, she provided herself with a small wand and began to push it about among the grasses and twigs and small stones which littered the path in the shrubberies.

After a long time of pushing and poking about she uttered a low exclamation and, taking from her handbag a small pair of tweezers and brushing some dead leaves aside with her wand, she picked up and laid on a flat stone — a poison dart.

Her flesh crept at sight of it, and she trembled to think she was standing exactly where Inez must have stood when she heard the faint whirr of the thing as it passed narrowly beside her leg.

She must have been waiting a second and fatal dart when the gun killed.

She was pleased by her piece of deduction but dared not risk leaving the dart: as sure as she did, some little wretch from the School would come and sit down on it. She tweezered it into a firmly closing tin box which she had in her bag.

There seemed to be no one about. Yet on reaching the hut she found herself challenged, and that unmistakably. Who should be emerging at the precise moment of her arrival but — Mr. Turtle.

Relations between Olive and Mr. Turtle had never improved. The mere sight of Olive in the distance set his beard angrily jerking, such teeth as he had little less than gnashing. Not that Mr. Turtle was a woman-hater — very far from it; but he did most profoundly believe that 'an 'ooman 'as 'er place'.

'Good morning, Mr. Turtle.'

'Mornin'.'

Nobody knows what it cost Mr. Turtle to say even so much.

Olive sought around for light conversation.

'Our friend doesn't seem to come back,' she remarked of the late occupant of the hut.

The lightness of her tone stung Mr. Turtle to renewed bitterness. But the bitterness forced him to speak.

'Which per'aps you will kindly explain your meanin', if an honest man may ventur'?'

'I meant the young man that used to live here — your assistant, wasn't he?'

'My assistant!' repeated Mr. Turtle on a note of rising choler. 'An' 'oo told you 'e was my assistant? A furriner 'e was.'

And here Mr. Turtle's innate tendency to philosophy betrayed him: his senior years, his dignity, his very manhood required of him that he now pass hence and leave Olive to her shame. But his desire to explore the depths of truth got the better of him.

'Assistant, ses you! A furriner! If there's two things,' said Mr. Turtle, 'on this 'ere revolvin' globe as I 'ates and detests, the one is a furriner, and the other is an 'ooman out of 'er place.'

'You don't die of your complaint,' Olive said, nodding her head. 'It's called 'xenophobia'. You seem to suffer rather badly.'

She had scored. If he had a fancy it was for polysyllables; he had come like most great philosophers to see that without these, and a generally inverted and periphrastic manner of speech, there could be no true philosophy. But he took Olive up on another point.

'I am not a man as suffers from nothink. Last time as I was taken with a turn, like, on account of doin' too much for others — which small is my reward — doctor ses when he examines me, ses he, 'Mr. Turtle,' ses doctor, 'there ain't a finer man for your time of life livin', and that I will tell you, 'ses doctor, 'to your face.' So 'oo may you be,' went on Mr. Turtle, to Olive, 'to set yourself up against doctor and tell me as I suffers from a complaint? Ah,' said Mr. Turtle, 'it comes to t'other thing as I was a-saying of — an 'ooman out of 'er place.'

Olive had contrived meanwhile to edge her way into the hut and to begin yet a further search among its scanty effects. But she had not forgotten Mr. Turtle.

'You interest me enormously, Mr. Turtle,' she said. 'If you're not too busy — and I know how little time you ever have for yourself — I wish you would tell me what in your opinion a woman's place *is*. But I expect you're too busy.'

But Mr. Turtle, though he scorned to show it, was touched. He suddenly saw Olive as a very young woman — nice-looking too — who, if she had erred and gone very far astray, had yet kept alive within her that most womanly of all feelings which consists in the desire to be instructed — to be instructed by man.

'Busy I will not deny that I am, miss,'

Mr. Turtle said, re-entering the hut and beginning to walk about with short heavy strides, 'and much I 'ave on me mind. But I am one 'oo was never so busy but wot I would find time some'ow when it was for the sake of another's need. Early on in life I ses to myself, like, 'Turtle,' I ses, 'of what use are you if you 'ides your light under a bushel?' and I resolves, miss, never so to do, and never 'ave I done. A woman's place, miss,' he added, with simple sublimity, 'is the 'ome.'

Olive made a gurgling noise which might have been interpreted in many ways. Mr. Turtle heard in it the hallelujah of the Methodist convert; he heard in it a sudden conviction of sin. His heart enlarged within his bosom — and not the less because he was struck again with Olive's charms.

'I couldn't agree with you more,' Olive said. 'But how if she hasn't got a home?'

It is absurd to suppose that such a philosopher as Mr. Turtle would have no answer to such an elementary question.

'If an 'ooman is so unfortnat, miss, as not to 'ave a 'ome — either the 'ome she was born in or the 'ome where she come as a sparkling bride — she cannot do better for 'erself than like the ladies up at 'ouse, and be resigned in the Lord. For the Lord, miss — the Lord —'

But at this point Mr. Turtle came a heavy stumble, threw up his arms and disappeared altogether from sight.

Olive rushed to his aid, for his groans were very pitiable. An excitement was upon her. Could it be that, in spite of Mother Assistant's positive answers to the contrary, there yet was a cellar under that hut? Cellar or no cellar, the floor had mysteriously given way under Mr. Turtle, and, looking down, Olive could see him lying in what seemed a catacomb.

Mr. Turtle had fallen in, giving himself a shock, but Olive, clearing away a little debris, jumped in beside him with no shock at all — except from Mr. Turtle's restless boots. He was in a very poor way, being convinced that his spine was broken. 'Ah, I might 'a known 'e'd get me in the end, that there furriner. Dead I am, and buried.'

'No, you aren't, Mr. Turtle dear,' Olive

reassured him. 'You're no more dead than I am. You only got a bit of a shock. Look what a nice little place we're in. He may have been very wicked, but he was clever, that foreigner of yours. He must have found there was a cave under his house. Look at the rug — and the pillow — and the little stove — and the — and the —' But she broke off.

'What's all *this*?' she cried.

Mr. Turtle, though suffering from fracture of the spine, followed her gaze, feeling pity for the weakness which had to ask such a question.

'That, miss?' he said. 'Why, it's nothink but a lot o' waste paper. It might 'a been useful for somethink but that it's all covered over with one o' them furrin laniges as don't mean nothink —'

Olive with shining eyes was picking up paper after paper. 'You've got it in one, Mr. Turtle. Really you're a wonderful man. There's something in the masculine mind —'

Mr. Turtle began to show distinct signs of recovery. He pulled at his whiskers and beamed at Olive.

Olive was sorting out the sheets. The language upon all of them was wildly beyond her, she could make neither head nor tail of it, but some of the sheets were of School exercise paper, and she guessed the writing to be that of Inez.

The only English she found appeared to be a page torn out of a railway time-table, dealing with trains to the New Forest.

She gathered up the papers and put them into her bag. The sooner she was gone now, the better. She knew there was a hiding-place under the hut. She had the dart. In the papers she had a treasure which might prove a solution of the mystery.

If only she could get the writing translated —

She suddenly thought of the Convent's Gaelic expert, Mother McVehoy. Mother McVehoy was said to be a genius at languages —

Meanwhile, there was the profound psychological task of getting Mr. Turtle to move. He had lighted his pipe and was looking extremely comfortable and only wanting another good go at philosophy.

'Well, I'm afraid I shall have to leave you, Mr. Turtle,' Olive said. 'I hate to do it, because after that shock you ought to get home and lie down. But of course not even a man as strong-minded as you could be expected to do that without help. I'll send help to you the first minute I can.'

''Elp,' said Mr. Turtle, 'is wot I never needed, miss, excep' the self-'elp of me manly mind.'

'Splendid, Mr. Turtle. That's what I should have expected. But no mind, however manly, could possibly just get up after a shock like yours and be at the door the same time as me. Why, you'll be telling me next that you're going to do a bit of work this morning!'

'That, miss, might be rash, considerin' the state of me spine. But where gettin' 'ome is concerned, and makin' myself comf'able and takin' the best care of meself, you can rely on me self-'elp.'

And Olive felt she could.

26

'It is a Terrible Responsibility, Reverend Mother — '

Days passed, much was done, but nothing was heard of Inez.

Anaconda, however, appeared on the map.

No longer had Reverend Mother to search in obscure columns of *The Times* for the information she wanted. Such information was to be had in many newspapers now, and usually on the front page. No sooner was Don Magnifiguo in power again than he made a striking gesture of affection and goodwill towards this country.

'Henceforth,' he cried, 'we in Anaconda shall look to great England for our manners and customs, our institutions and ideals.'

England was naturally rather pleased. It is always pleasant to have somebody's good opinion, especially when one has been at no trouble to obtain it, and no expense at all.

Editors did not fail to draw attention to the very undictatorial amnesty proclaimed by the victor in Anaconda.

The tables were now turned: it was not now Reverend Mother who anxiously rang up Sir Clement de Willowby about Inez, it was Sir Clement de Willowby himself who came to the Convent and, refusing to wait until Mother Peck had ascertained what Reverend Mother's engagements were, strode straight to the Parlour.

Hardly giving Reverend Mother time to express her pleasure at seeing him, and profoundly disedifying Mother Peck by abstractedly shutting the door in her face, he plunged *in medias res*.

'What's all this I hear? You can't find Inez? Do you realize her father is coming to see her?'

Reverend Mother nodded. 'I thought he might.'

Sir Clement refused to sit down, he strode the room with immense strides.

'And you mean to tell me that Scotland Yard — that all you clever ladies — you haven't an idea between you?'

'Scotland Yard is doing its best. As for us, we are only nuns — not mediums or soothsayers. And oh yes, there are plenty of ideas. The best is from one of the children — a senior girl, no fool, and she says she had it from Inez herself. Inez has reverted to the jungle.'

'You said the girl was no fool. Revert to the jungle indeed! How can she revert to what doesn't exist?'

'Inez believes it does. She cannot imagine a great country without a jungle. And so I suppose she has gone to look for it.'

'I must say,' Sir Clement said, 'you seem to take it with 'more than usual calm'.'

'We are all praying,' was the answer.

'Yes. Oh yes, of course.'

'Not at all. I only wish it were. The fact remains, however, that God knows where the child is and will show us if we trustfully ask Him.'

'And I meanwhile,' said Sir Clement,

'have got to draft an answer to her father!'

'Is that so difficult? Surely it is not beyond the wit of the Foreign Office to word a complimentary telegram?'

'And what about Inez?'

'What about Inez? I don't think I should say anything — not at present —'

'And suppose he says he is coming at once?'

'Really,' Reverend Mother said, 'you people of little faith are rather pathetic.'

'It is a terrible responsibility, Reverend Mother.'

'It is one I am perfectly prepared to take. Leave it to me. I am the person chiefly responsible to Inez's father, and, if the necessity arises, I will be answerable. If you wish to delay his coming I will word the telegram. But if I were you I should let things be.'

'Take the risk?' Sir Clement sat down on a chair beside Reverend Mother and searched her eye. 'Are you sure you haven't got some clue — some clue which you're keeping back from me?' he said.

'If I had a clue,' she replied, 'such a clue as would set your mind at rest at once, I would tell you. But though I have a — sort of — clue, and a clue based on some evidence, I feel inclined to keep it to myself for the present. I shall only say now that I have had many long talks with Inez, in which she used to tell me a great deal about herself, and I used sometimes to amuse her with stories about myself. It is possible,' Reverend Mother went on after a pause, 'that when the poor child was frantic for a hiding-place, one of my stories — which were true stories — may have come into her mind.'

'When,' cried Sir Clement, 'will you be able to go into this?'

'I have gone some distance into it already. I have made sure of some points. You, Sir Clement, might be able to help me very much —'

'I'll do any mortal thing.'

'You haven't by any chance at the Foreign Office an expert in the — Anacondan language?'

'In the Anacondan language!' Sir Clement threw up his hands. 'Believe me, there 'isn't no sich a person'. Certainly there isn't in the F.O.'

'Oh well, it doesn't matter. We have a nun here already well ahead.'

'A nun — already well ahead —' Sir Clement gasped it.

Reverend Mother spoke with quiet pride.

'Yes. And she had nothing to go on but the Four Gospels as translated into Anacondan by the original Jesuit missionaries. These were found in Inez's cubicle. Yet within a week Mother McVehoy was able to translate a correspondence in Anacondan which explained the whole of this case. We know now what happened to Inez, and how she was saved. We know how this Diego hid himself and how he kept in touch. We know, though it is all but unbelievable, how he got her out of the house on the night it was attacked. It remains now to see where he took her.'

'And what, if I may ask,' said Sir Clement, 'does this prodigy of yours — this woman who can learn Anacondan in a week — do with herself in a general way?'

'Oh, Mother McVehoy? Well, she takes all the Senior French —'

'Schoolgirl French! A woman like that! Why, she ought to be a professor in a university —'

'Well,' said Reverend Mother, 'she was.'

'Was?' cried Sir Clement, eating his moustache. 'Why isn't she now?'

'Well, she still writes books — and reads a paper now and then to some learned society. But you see,' said Reverend Mother in almost an apologetic voice, 'she found she had a vocation.'

'Pshaw!' cried Sir Clement, springing to his feet.

And fond as he was of Reverend Mother, and long as it was since he had seen her, no persuasions of hers could get him to stay to tea.

27

Reverend Mother Takes a Day Off

Mother Peck, putting her head in at Reverend Mother's parlour next morning, almost received a stumbling-block.

Reverend Mother, actually Reverend Mother, was practising, under the tuition of Mother McVehoy, how to make the key-sound of Anacondan, which is called the 'sacred aspirate'.

'Excellent, Reverend Mother — excellent.' (Reverend Mother had just made a sound in her throat which Mother Peck would hardly have liked to characterize.)

'If you will pardon my saying so,' went on Mother McVehoy, 'I think you want to make more use of the *uvula*. You know — that small process which depends from the back of the palate —'

'Yes. I know the thing. I have never at all cared for the look of it. How clever of you to call it a 'process'. Is that what it is?'

'A fleshy process,' said Mother McVehoy (causing Mother Peck's hair to stand almost upright in her bonnet).

'Dear me,' said Reverend Mother, and used her uvula to such effect that a perfect sacred aspirate was the result.

But Mother Peck could contain herself no longer.

'Excuse me, dear Reverend Mother, but if I may interrupt your learned pursuits a moment — that young police lady, Miss Churston, I believe her name is, has come begging for a moment of your time. I have pointed out that your engagements make this wholly impossible. But she still persists. May I ask you to make your refusal quite plain?'

'Oh dear no, Mother; you can't do that,' exclaimed Reverend Mother in reply. 'Miss Churston in fact *is* my main engagement for today. Go and make my apologies and beg her to join us here.'

Olive crept in a moment later looking very timid.

'I thought you must have changed your mind about going today, Reverend Mother. Mother Peck assured me that you hadn't a free moment —'

'You must not believe quite *all* Mother Peck says about me.'

'Oh, I don't. I mean — I beg your pardon —'

'It is 'Zeal, Mr. Easy',' quoted Reverend Mother. 'And now, dear, have you got us a nice car to go in and a really good driver?'

'The car is all right,' Olive said. 'It's the best at the station. It's Oliver's — I mean the Superintendent's — but when he heard it was you he lent it at once.'

Reverend Mother smiled and patted Olive's shoulder.

'Please give him my best thanks. Wasn't he the officer who went upstairs with Mr. MacTavish when they might have been blown to pieces?'

'Yes. And he was first in the chapel after you and Mother Assistant —'

'He is — a friend of yours?'

Olive's eyes were downcast as she answered.

'Yes, Reverend Mother.'

'And would like to be something more, eh? Well, tell him your Reverend Mother gives her permission. And now about the driver?'

'The driver is me.'

'My child. And you have such slender arms. Does Oliver really approve of this?'

'Well, it's his car. And he taught me to drive — and he always lets me drive when I go out with him —'

'And you have taken the driving-test?'

'One has to, you know, Reverend Mother. Whatever should I as a policeman have to say to myself?'

'Well, I shall be delighted, my dear.' And Reverend Mother put her hand on Olive's shoulder.

Quite a crowd of nuns and children had gathered to see Reverend Mother off. Mother Assistant was there, and Torquilla. Mother Peck was in an equal state of deference and exultation — deference for Reverend Mother, and exultation that for once her conscience would be perfectly clear in. asserting against all comers, Reverend Mother's engagements were such *she could not be seen.*

The day, though it was well into

November, promised to be fair, and Reverend Mother, settling down beside Olive, was her perfectly charming, if ever-detached, self.

'How well you drive, my dear. What a great many things your generation does which ours did not. I wonder which has the best of it — really?'

'Yours,' Olive said. 'It had the horse.'

'So it had. One did not go so far but so much more pleasantly, seeing all that was to be seen, and taking the very best exercise all the time. Then one got so fond of a horse.'

'Used you to do a great deal of riding?' Olive asked.

'I was as seldom off a horse's back,' said Reverend Mother, smiling, 'as possible. I should have liked to be a centaur.'

Olive would have liked to hear more, but Reverend Mother sat silent until after a while Olive was startled to hear beside her a very correct and even beautiful rendering of the sacred aspirate.

Reverend Mother owned up at once.

'Yes, I did it. Did you think it good?'

'Perfect,' Olive said.

Reverend Mother looked pleased.

'I find it quite easy when Mother McVehoy isn't telling me how. I was always like that, I am afraid. When people start being scientific about things, talking about 'uvulas' and 'fleshy processes' and so on, I am hopeless.'

She went on:

'I am glad you thought it good, because, you know, we have definitely got to find Inez today. If we don't her father may arrive in her absence, and that would be so terribly disappointing for him.'

'I only hope we shall,' Olive said, feeling, however, very slight confidence.

Soon afterwards they arrived at the charming little New Forest town of Lyndhurst.

28

'Grace'

Olive's spirits suffered a further declension as, entering the town, she drew up at a corner of the market-place.

Owing to the fine weather there were many people in the streets and good business being done in the shops. There were cars in plenty, telling of the well-populated neighbourhood all about. Every corner directed to some part of the Forest, and Olive could not see that Inez was likely to be in one more than another. Certainly she and Reverend Mother could not hope to visit more than a few.

'Where had we better go now?' she inquired rather disconsolately of Reverend Mother. 'There are such heaps of ways.'

'And all so well worth visiting,' said Reverend Mother, rather with the air of a tripper visiting the Forest for the first time.

Olive looked at her almost with hostility. There were times when Reverend Mother's detachment could be very aggravating.

'Yes. But what about Inez?' Olive said.

'Don't worry about her, dear. If she is here at all, I think we shall be guided to the right place.'

'Yes. But hadn't we better be setting about it? The days are not very long in November.'

'No, they are not, are they? We are getting along to the shortest day and Christmas. Do you know, my dear, I think I shall go into the back of the car and eat my sandwiches. I should advise you to do the same in front.' So saying, she gave Olive a neat little packet of sandwiches and a small Thermos, herself retiring to the back with the same.

When Reverend Mother had finished her lunch — and she was in no hurry — she packed away the paper and the flasks in her bag again.

'Well,' she said, 'I think we might be

going. Myself, I have a fancy for the Lymington road. Long ago when I was a little girl and used to drive about here with my grandmother I was always glad when she chose the Lymington road. It was a charming drive in the direction of Lymington — in the old days of carriages and horses. I should be glad to do it again — after all these years —'

Olive kept her temper with difficulty.

'But — but is the Lymington road the best for finding Inez?' she said, almost fretfully.

'Oh, I should think so. I shouldn't wonder. We mustn't go fast, or I shall miss all the old places. My grandmother used to use a victoria, and I sat up beside the coachman dangling my legs.'

A glance at Reverend Mother's profile as they took the Lymington road revealed nothing but perfect tranquillity and pleased anticipation.

'Why can't she speak outright?' Olive chafed.

'A lovely day for this time of the year,' Reverend Mother was murmuring.

'Really — these nuns —!'

Olive drove slowly and sulkily along the road to Lymington, Reverend Mother sitting up very straight beside her and missing no feature of the way. Again and again she exclaimed at the beauty of the country and commented on some incident of her own childhood.

'It was just here the coachman would always inquire if Grandmamma wished to turn back. Oh, how I did hope she would say no. But little girls were not asked what they would like in those days. Really, dear, if you don't mind, I think I should like to get out here for a moment and breathe the air again.'

Olive drew up and opened the door for Reverend Mother. She was thinking:

'By all means have a breath of the air. It's what we seem to have come for. It will help the time nicely on until we have to go back.'

Reverend Mother, now outside the car, was renewing her youth.

'Dear me, what an adventure! Grandmamma was very strict. There was no moving her —'

'Just such another as yourself,' Olive

was thinking. 'Like grandmother, like grandchild. Where on earth is she going now?'

Reverend Mother was across the road and sauntering off into a glade.

'Come with me.' She called back.

'I shall do nothing of the sort!' Olive thought. But in fact she got out at once and pursued Reverend Mother.

'I'm getting like Mother Peck,' she scolded herself.

Reverend Mother waited for Olive to catch up. Her smile had never been so charming.

'Don't be cross with me, my dear. I am not forgetting business in my pleasure.'

'Oh, you're not!' Olive thought. 'My mistake!'

'You see,' Reverend Mother was saying, gently strolling with Olive by the arm, 'I used to be acquainted with these parts — oh dear me, ever so many years ago. We are a Hampshire family. My grandfather retired here and became the Lord-Lieutenant of the county when I was a little girl.'

'You're coming to the point sometime,

I suppose,' Olive thought, though she was thrilled to have even so much information about the incarnate detachment at her side.

'And so,' Reverend Mother proceeded, 'when little Inez used to tell me about the jungle I sometimes put in a good word for the New Forest. I described this particular part in some detail, because it is where my brothers and I used to play. In fact we had a little summer-house farther on. I believe it has been turned into a bungalow for my brother's children and their children in the summer.'

She slightly quickened her step.

'Inez *may* have remembered,' she said. 'At any rate, I thought it worth trying. The property,' she added, 'still belongs to the family, and I believe my brother has made rather a point of keeping it private. After all, why not? He has served his country very well. Of course I am prejudiced, but I do think landowners are entitled to keep a little.'

'And you've had all this inside that bonnet of yours all this time!' Olive thought. She was now intensely excited.

Reverend Mother went on quietly speaking.

'However, that is not the point. I mention it because if those two did come here it was open and waiting for them. It is well stocked with tinned foods and cereals. There is water to be had close at hand. And,' she added, 'here is the place.'

As she spoke a turn in the wooded aisle where they were walking revealed the bungalow. Or perhaps hardly revealed it, for it was small and low-lying, made of wood, and painted so as to assort with its surroundings. It might very easily have been passed by and never noticed.

Reverend Mother was explaining.

'In the old days,' she said, 'when it was just a playhouse for children, it was called 'Grace's Rainproof' — after me. My name is Grace. It did not matter for my brothers when it rained, but I had to take care of my frocks. Ah,' she broke off, as she advanced to the little gate in the fence, 'it is still called by the old name. How it comes over the years. He was always the dearest and kindest of brothers.'

An almost unearthly silence brooded around, like the silence which falls upon a garden when bedtime ends the play of happy children. Olive was subdued. Reverend Mother seemed entranced.

'What shall we do?' Olive whispered.

Reverend Mother did not reply: instead, standing where she was by the little gate, she clearly and perfectly sounded the sacred aspirate.

'Inez,' she gently called, 'Inez —'

Nothing happened. Not an old leaf quivered of the many about to fall. Olive could have imagined that the silence was being held by some force.

'Inez —' called Reverend Mother.

Then there was a sound. From behind them, an almost inaudible stir.

Reverend Mother did not turn round, but Olive did. And there, sure enough, stood a young man whom she recognized at once, from the descriptions and the photographs she had seen, to be the man called Juan Copanza.

He spoke to her in French.

'Pardon, ma'moiselle, if I make trespass. It was not my intention. I was passing by and I see the little house —'

'Will you not speak to Reverend Mother?' Olive said, also in French.

'I will not intrude. I will go now. A thousand pardons —'

But Reverend Mother had turned round.

'Diego,' she said, 'where is the señorita?'

But still he kept it up.

'Pardon, madame. But perhaps there is some little error. I would very gladly serve you, but I am a stranger in these parts — in this England. It is impossible that I am a person madame would know.'

'Perhaps,' replied Reverend Mother, 'there is no error at all. Perhaps you know who I am and what I have come about as well as I do. You have done very well, Diego. But there is no more reason for disguise. All the danger is past. You have committed no crime. I have come to fetch the señorita because,' her voice rose to gentle command, 'her father is coming to see her.'

But his face showed not a sign.

'I do not understand —'

'Yes, you do, Diego. Be quick now and do what I tell you.'

He would have denied again. But now it mattered little whether he did or no, for another's ear had overheard Reverend Mother's words, and another's voice made answer.

'*Oh, Reverend Muzzer. Did you say my fazzer is coming? Did you say my fazzer?*'

And Inez stood, glowing, beside them.

29

In the End

Glowing!

That was the word which described Inez.

The single glance which Reverend Mother gave her showed that the sun had not struck her by day, neither the moon by night. Clean, kempt, well dressed, she had fed well and slept well during her *villegiatura*.

Now here she was in perfect health, spirits and beauty.

'Well, my child. So here you are.'

'Oh, Reverend Muzzer, how you guess? My fazzer — it is true he come?'

'Yes, dear, he is coming. As to guessing, I thought you would perhaps remember 'Grace' and the little house which was built for her among the trees.'

'But — of course. Oh, it was lovely to be living in the little house. I think so much of 'Grace'. Sometimes I almost see her, but not quite. She has a mystery, that girl —'

'Come and let us walk round the little house, Inez. I may not come inside, but I may look through the windows and remember.'

'Oh yes, Reverend Muzzer, let us.'

When they were gone, Diego, who had held apart in silence, approached Olive and spoke.

'Pardon, lady, but you are the police, is it not?'

Olive found herself flushing, and most unwilling to make the admission.

'I am — connected — with the police. But — I am not on duty just now.'

He looked crestfallen.

'Perhaps you — become on duty — if I tell you I am the gardener-man Juan Copanza, which is 'wanted' by de police for shooting de man on de dump.'

'I am afraid I must warn you,' Olive said, and got out her notebook, 'that anything you say about that may be taken down and used against you.'

'So I t'ink,' he replied. 'But yet I wish

to say that I kill that man. I do so because he has tried to kill other person, and is about to try again.'

Olive made notes. 'Can you remember the day of this, and where it was? And your name? And the other person's name? And if your name is not Juan Copanza do not say it is.'

He gave what Olive knew to be the right answers as to date, time and place. The 'other person' was, of course, Inez. But he hesitated and seemed most unwilling to give his right name.

'I have heard Inez call you Diego,' Olive said.

'Perhaps I am what you call 'snob',' he replied. 'Perhaps I do not like to work as Spanish gardener boy under de old Turtle. I am not Spaniard but Anacondan; and my name is Diego del Sagrad y Sole.'

There was a pause while Olive wrote down the name, and then she said:

'You needn't answer my questions, Don Diego. I ask them because I wish you very well. But why did you call yourself Juan Copanza?'

'Dear lady, to disguise myself. It is of the highest importance that I am unknown. So I give myself de name of a servant which I have, which is real Spaniard, and I borrow from him the diplomas and certificates he has, of excellence, and so I am able to apply under old Turtle.'

'But you didn't come here to be a gardener under old Turtle?' Olive suggested gently.

'I come here, lady, to protect and to guard over de Señorita Inez. Her father choose me for dis greatest and sweetest of all honours because it is arranged, when she grow older, and if I can gain her love, we are to be married.'

'You will have a very pretty little bride,' Olive said, liking the young man all the better for the ecstatic solemnity of his tone.

'Lady, you speak but the truth. And yet how kind are your words. May I ask if the sentence in prison is very long for killing?'

'Not for such killing as yours, Don Diego. It was homicide, I suppose, but not in any sense murder, or manslaughter. I think any judge would direct it was 'justifiable homicide',

'I thought,' Diego said, 'if I put de brown paper on de body that would make it all right. In Anaconda de brown paper mean it is a murderer which has been killed. In Anaconda it is twice and three times to be a murderer to shoot with the poison blowgun.'

'I am not surprised. But don't you think your best plan both for Inez and yourself would have been to tell Reverend Mother the whole story and let her take steps to protect you both?'

'I do not know if she will believe me. I am, after all, only the gardener. Before I know I am almost off my head. So nearly dey succeed. I cannot keep in touch with Inez. I am in peril also of my own life. Not that I mind this for myself, but if I am dead my beloved also will die. No, lady, no: your scheme to tell all to de Reverend Mother break down at every point.'

'I think what you did was marvellous,' Olive said.

'God bless de sweet soul of her. She is standing,' he cried, 'like dis — ' And he perfectly acted the child's expectation of instant death. 'And dat man, which is also a snake, is crouching, crouching right down on de ground, preparing his second dart. Dis I see, lady, all at a glance. I know dat nothing can save her but dis man's destruction. Is he a man? I cry out to alarm him and make him again blow wrong. His back is towards me, and I shoot into him — where I know it will kill — two bullets — zip, zip — '

Olive found herself shaking with relief.

'Is — is it — painful, the poison?'

'For a moment, lady — agony — '

He told Olive then how he had taken Inez up to the house, keeping her in among the bushes, trying to comfort her, to explain to her his plans which she was too utterly dazed to understand.

'De nun is very cross, and I see Inez crying. My heart is quite broken. But as I go away a gentle voice speak in my ear. It is dat Sister Ursula, and she say, 'I guess dere is danger for Miss Inez, and you are on her side.' I deny at first, but I am so lonely and so mis'able I tell a little. And de Sister say, 'I also am on her side, and on your side, and all I can do to help I will do.'

'And so it is arranged between us — the Sister Ursula and myself.

'And de Sister is good as her word. It is she dat come to my hut in de dark and fog and danger to tell me dey have moved Inez to de New Building. And she never betray dat I am hidden at my hut, but bring food whenever she can.

'She warn me to come and wait outside de New Building until I see a light at a window.

'Dere is a great fire in the chapel, and all de nuns are needed to put it out. So Sister Ursula go quick to de nun which is with Inez, and she say, 'Why do you not also go to de fire? I will stay with de child.' And de detectives see what is done, but dey do not understand.

'So when de door is closed again, de Sister go quietly, quietly to de window, and she open de shutter and show a small light, which I see.

'Dere is a tree which I am upon. When

I see de light I spring from my tree to de building and climb up to de window.

'De Sister have a rope. Inez is all ready, and de Sister hold de rope while I slide down it with Inez to de ground.

'When we are gone for some time,' added Diego, 'de Sister is going to take some medicine which de doctor give Inez. It will make her unconscious at first, and then forgetful for a long while.'

'Wasn't that a bit hard on Reverend Mother?' Olive said. 'She must have thought the worst had happened.'

'No. For Inez write little note. *I am safe. Inez.* And now if you will be so kind you will tell if de Reverend Muzzer was very angry with de Sister? For dat has made Inez and me very unhappy for fear.'

'No. Reverend Mother wasn't angry. She guessed what had happened — '

'Dat Inez go off with de gardener?' This was a very sore point with Don Diego.

But Olive shook her head. 'Don't you believe it. The Sister was very strong on that. She said you were a very high hidalgo who had pretended to be a gardener so as to come here and look after Inez. She said you were noble, good and brave — '

'Bless her. I am none of these t'ings. But I am certainly a del Sagrad y Sole. I am not — how does he so abominably call hisself? — a Turtle.' And at this point Diego burst out laughing.

'Pardon, dear lady, dat I laugh so much, but how can I help when I t'ink how you give dis old Turtle de good tickle off — '

Olive found him entirely charming; he was gay, ingenuous and debonair, dividing his eager speech between the glory which was Inez and the grandeur which was the New Anaconda,

'You also, dear lady — will you not come to de New Anaconda? I cannot describe to you de beauty of dat country or de excellence of de humane institutions which de Hazh Bazh design. Dere is nuzzing which would give him so more pleasure dan de refined observations of English lady — if she would give some talks perhaps about how t'ings are done in England. Oh,' cried Diego, 'I feel if once you have seen de jungle, never will you wish to absent youself from its fascinations. Imagine seeing a python of twenty-five feet long!'

'And imagine it seeing me!' Olive thought.

But Diego got well away on the subject of 'de excellence of de New Institutions', which, if they could be carried out, did really sound like a measure of freedom for poor old Anaconda with its hapless past of squalid tyranny. Certainly Diego meant what he was saying, and so, Olive believed, did the Hazh Bazh too. There was no doubting his goodwill. If it all sounded a bit like 'compulsoey games', that in the beginning was inevitable; there would be less 'compulsion' and more 'games' as time went on.

'We cannot all at once do without de Hazh Bazh,' said Diego, 'but we can learn, and de Hazh Bazh is determined himself to learn. He aspires to a time when he can be de President of de Republic of Anaconda. Meanwhile he wish that great and high English people, like yourself, dear lady, shall come as guest to Anaconda and show how

Freedom is done.'

Olive was not at all inclined to laugh: an idea had come into her head.

'I should love to come to Anaconda,' she said, 'and meet Inez's family, which sounds so charming. But I don't think I know enough to talk to people and teach about methods of government — but I know someone, far more important than me, who does. It's a man, not a woman; and a man high in his profession — which is the practical side of the law.'

She hesitated, flushed a little, and went on:

'I — I am going to marry him.'

She went on quicker than ever:

'I — I have an idea — if the Hazh Bazh asked the Foreign Office — *they* could get Scotland Yard to second a commissioned police officer to come out for a while and help the Hazh Bazh. I — think my man — would rather like it. — Only,' she suddenly broke off, 'for goodness' sake don't take him into jungles — '

Diego swept her an operatic bow.

'Now will de Hazh Bazh de indeed a proud and happy man — to have a great

Englishman and a beautiful English-woman to spend deir honeymoon with him in Anaconda! Now is de freedom of Anaconda assured. De Hazh Bazh will do what your husband say, de people will do what de Hazh Bazh say, and at once we shall have London in Lilitha!'

They could have gone on indefinitely but that Olive at this moment was hugged round the waist by Inez and the voice of Reverend Mother was heard in the land.

Inez never missed an opportunity of showing off her accomplishments before Reverend Mother, and so she dropped a curtsey and said:

'Il faut partir, monsieur et ma'moiselle.'

'C'est dommage, n'est-ce pas?' said Reverend Mother.

'And oh,' Olive cried, 'how dark it's got. I shall never be back in time — and I faithfully promised Oliver to have dinner with him — '

Diego also saw the necessity of haste. 'You must indeed keep such an appointment' — and picking up Inez, whom it had had now become his habit to carry, he vanished at a run in the direction of the car.

'It is a pity the same thing cannot be done for me,' said Reverend Mother to Olive. ' 'Grace' would have been there first, and scolded for romping.' She paused for a last look at the little house. 'Well, I never thought to be back here again. It just shows. To think that at my age I should be stepping out like this over bumpy ground — '

She stepped out, continuing to speak:

'They say nuns are inhuman. But I shall miss that child every hour of the day. I like Diego, and think they will be very happy in a year or two. They have similar natures — so ingenuous and affectionate.'

'It is a very pretty ending,' Olive said. 'But oh, Reverend Mother, shouldn't we thank God for pistols when we think of the — unspeakable beginning — '

'One should always thank God,' Reverend Mother said.

She added, after a pause:

'I suppose Diego will be in no trouble?'

'An inquiry, I should suppose. Sir Andrew Pearson will attend to it.'

'God bless him,' said Reverend Mother.

Olive began to speak hurriedly.

'Oh — and, Reverend Mother, there was something I rather wanted to tell you — '

'Was there, dear? Tell me then.'

'You remember the — man I mentioned — our local Superintendent, who went up those stairs with Mr. MacTavish and was first in the chapel after you and Mother Assistant — well, I always liked him — he's utterly different from other men, if you see what I mean — well, he hung back and wouldn't push, and — I thought he didn't care, and perhaps I was meant to be a nun. Anyhow, everything got cleared up, and now we're engaged. And — and the Hazh Bazh is going to try to have Oliver seconded out there for a time, to give lectures and instructions and form a nucleus of police — and he really is a marvellous speaker, Reverend Mother. And oh, I do hope you will like him.'

'Surely, dear, the great thing is that you do.'

'Oh, Reverend Mother, don't be horrid — '

'My child, as one loving *you*, I have dared to have several talks with Oliver, and — '

'*And?*'

'I bless and congratulate you, Olive dear, with all my heart.'

Other titles in the
Linford Mystery Library:

FROST LINE

Ardath Mayhar and
Mary Wickizer Burgess

A helpless woman is attacked in her home by a ruthless gang of murderers and thieves searching for her brother's valuable gun collection. They fail in their mission, and now they're coming back to finish the job — this time determined to leave no eye witnesses alive. Sheriff Washington Shipp must use all his instincts and expertise to track them down before they can strike again. But one of the criminals, more dangerous than all the rest, is leaving a trail of bodies across Louisiana — and Wash may be next in line . . .

LORD JAMES HARRINGTON AND THE CHRISTMAS MYSTERY

Lynn Florkiewicz

It's Christmas, and James and Beth are preparing for Harrington's festive dinner and dance. This year, famous diva Olivia Dupree is singing, a wedding is taking place, and they're hosting a reunion of Pals — ex-army comrades from the Great War. When Olivia falls ill and claims she's been poisoned, James puts his sleuthing hat on. But things take a sinister turn when a further attack occurs. What links the two victims? James must race against time to stop multiple murders taking place.